THE AZURE BACKLASH

MITCH HERRON 5

STEVE P. VINCENT

For Sam Vincent.

A bubbly and smiling addition to the world in one of the hardest times for it.

1

—————

Mitch Herron shouted to be heard over the waves that crashed against the hull of his yacht and the constant buzz of the oncoming Zodiac boat's engine. "Turn back!"

The man at the tiller of the Zodiac ignored his demands. The jet-black inflatable, bearing its quartet of thugs armed with firearms and blades, kept on course.

If they wouldn't turn their boat around voluntarily, Herron would have to give them some more forceful encouragement.

He levelled his pistol at the pilot, adjusted his aim for the rise and fall of the boat in the water, then fired. The pistol roared, the man slid over the side, and another took his place at the tiller. Herron sighed, irritated he had to kill to keep these men away from him, but they'd proven relentless, and the odds were stacked against him.

Herron pocketed the pistol, its ammo spent. He'd seen off the occupants of two previous boats, plus the man he'd just downed. Nine shots for nine kills was a range score anyone would be proud of, but here in the real world he now faced three more armed assailants without the firepower to defend himself from range.

The hijackers seemed to realise he was out of ammo, because when no further shots boomed at them, they let out visceral howls of victory. They thought they had him cold, a lone sailor trapped in the middle of the ocean. They didn't know Herron had made a career of killing far more dangerous threats than them.

Herron gripped the yacht's wheel as the Zodiac thudded against the hull and, a second later, the first grappling hook flew over the side and caught against a rail. Teeth clenched in his determination to stop them getting aboard, he reached out for the throttle and pushed it to full speed.

The engine roared in response, and he spun the wheel back-and-forth aggressively, to no effect. One thug appeared over the side. Then another. Then the third.

His evasive manoeuvres foiled, Herron let go of the wheel and pulled back on the throttle. Now he'd have to do it the hard way.

He crouched down and reached into the safe inside the life jacket compartment, still unlocked from retrieving the pistol. He came out with a few stacks of cash and a combat knife, put everything in his pockets, and locked the safe. Then he left the wheelhouse to confront the attackers.

"Don't shoot!" He shouted as he approached the hijackers with his hands up. "Please, I have money!"

"Anyone else on board?" The pirate closest to Herron spoke in broken English, a broad grin on his face. "Any more guns or other weapons?"

"No more guns and nobody else on board." Herron stopped ten yards from Smiley. "I've got cash in my pocket. I'll give it to you if you leave."

"You should have jumped overboard." Smiley laughed and took a few steps closer. "Now we're going to take your money, your boat *and* your life."

Herron's face remained expressionless, although he wanted to smile. When he'd seen the first Zodiac, he'd believed he could see the attack off; he'd still had confidence when he'd spotted the second. But the third was more than he could handle with a small yacht and a now-empty pistol. To have a chance, he'd need to get up close and personal, and Smiley was playing right into his hands.

He feigned fear. "Let me get the cash for you..."

"Slowly." Smiley waved his pistol at him. "If there's enough, we might let you jump after all."

Herron reached into his pocket, gripped a rolled-up wad of US dollars, and threw it underarm. As the cash soared through the air, Smiley and his two accomplices tracked its trajectory... which was exactly what Herron had hoped for. He dug into his pocket again.

And threw the knife right at Smiley.

It flew like a pitcher's fastball and buried itself in the hijacker's chest. As Smiley cried out, Herron closed the distance between them and pulled the knife free. A stream of blood came with it, but it was a trickle compared to the gush of crimson that washed over Herron as he slit the stunned man's throat.

With only a few seconds to capitalize on his advantage, Herron charged at the next closest hijacker and hit him like a line-backer. The crown of his head destroyed the man's jaw, the force of the impact knocking the pirate out. He sagged, and Herron lifted him over the side of the yacht.

He vanished over the rail without so much as a scream.

The last attacker yelled, and Herron turned in time to see a length of pipe en route to his head. Backed up against the guardrail, he blocked the blow with his forearm and grunted in pain as it hit, but a sore arm—perhaps even a fractured one—was better than a caved-in skull.

Arm throbbing, Herron spoke through gritted teeth. "I'm going to shove that pipe up your ass."

The hijacker's face flushed red, and he swung again. Herron lashed out with a strike to the throat, and the man stumbled backwards. The bar still hit Herron's head, but with a fraction of the force it would have otherwise. Herron shrugged off the blow and pressed forward.

When the next swing came, Herron caught the pipe, wrenched it from the pirate's hand, and went on the offensive. He whaled on the man, all his pent-up fury and frustration taken out on the one target he had left. Soon, the last hijacker was curled up in a foetal position, barely conscious.

Finished with the beating, Herron threw the pipe over the side of the boat and glared at the pirate. "I want to know how it feels."

The injured man groaned and rolled onto his side, his eyes wide. "How what feels?"

Herron kicked him. "To attack someone with twelve-to-one odds and still lose."

Behind Herron, a woman cleared her throat. "I think you mean sixteen-to-two."

Herron froze as a knife pressed into his neck. Clearly, a fourth group of attackers had come aboard while he was busy. But it was worse than that. A new sneering pirate stepped into view, dragging a young girl with him. She struggled and squirmed, but could not break his grip.

Lynda.

She should have been hidden below deck.

The daughter of a friend, she'd stowed away before Herron left Fiji, intent on using him as her ticket to see the world. He'd had no time to drop her off before the pirates had attacked—the best he could do was hide her and hope she'd stay put until the danger had passed.

But his best hadn't been good enough.

The taste of failure was bitter, but Herron hadn't survived in his profession by dwelling on mistakes or setbacks. He needed a new plan.

"Let her go." Herron paused, already regretting his next words. "I won't resist."

"No," Lynda yelled. "Don't let them–"

"This isn't a negotiation," interrupted the woman behind him, her blade unwavering at his throat. "If you resist, I'll skin your passenger alive."

"And if I don't?"

"She might live." A pause. "Even if you won't."

Herron sighed. "Deal."

* * *

THE WOMAN SLAPPED him hard across the face, then took a step back to survey her work. Blood flowed from Herron's nose and onto his bare chest, slick with spit and the blood she'd already spilled. Tied to a chair in the wheelhouse and unable to move, he let the pain recede, keeping his eyes locked on his torturer.

"I'm going to rip out your throat," he snarled. "I promise you."

"A lot of men have promised that, but do you know the one constant with them?" She laughed. "They're all dead."

Herron didn't respond. His mind was a clouded soup of pain and fatigue. In the hour since the woman and her hijackers had captured him, they'd kicked the crap out of him. No bones had been broken—yet—but he figured that'd be next if he didn't give them what they wanted.

The contents of his secret safe.

The woman could make all the threats she wanted, but that was something he would never give up. The safe contained his entire life—weapons, cash, identities, and cell phones. If he let her take it all, he'd be stateless and broke, an easy target for the law enforcement agencies and old enemies who were always just one step behind.

She chortled as she paced in front of him. "It's the thing I admire about the female widow spider. She gets what she needs from the males in her life and then disposes of them."

"Let me guess..." Herron snorted. "Your nickname is the Widow, and it impresses all your little hijacker friends?"

Her features hardened. She was a short woman, Chinese—if he had to guess—and about thirty-five, rock hard, without a curve to be seen. She had the cold eyes of a killer who took pride in her work, a dangerous foe who might live up to her nickname if he gave her the chance.

"Enough games." She leaned in close and stroked his cheek softly, her voice a whisper. "Tell me the safe code."

Herron kept his mouth shut, although it would mean more pain, a continuation of her bloody work. So far, none of his injuries were too serious, but they were painful and bloody enough to shake Herron. And it was clear she was just getting started.

"You're not getting the code." Herron's words were a mumble, but her laugh told him she'd heard him well enough. "What's funny?"

"I suggest you change your tone." The Widow turned to speak to one of the other hijackers in a language he didn't know, then turned back to Herron. "You know this can only end one way."

Herron shifted his gaze as the man left the wheelhouse, and a few moments later, Lynda was marched in with a knife to her throat. She was trying to be brave, her lips pursed together, but her eyes showed terror—wide and desperate, and locked onto him in a silent plea for help.

He'd first saved Lynda when she was a small child, taken by a sexual predator in Fiji and only moments from being assaulted. He'd helped her again less than a week ago, so he'd be damned if he was going to let her be hurt now.

The Widow was right. There was only one way out of the situation.

"It's okay." Herron forced a smile at Lynda, and when she returned it cautiously, he looked to the Widow. "The code for her safety?"

The Widow nodded at the hijacker, who removed the knife from Lynda's throat. Her smile, unlike Herron's and Lynda's, lacked all warmth. "You have my word."

"Seven. Four. One." Herron paused.

"No!" Lynda elbowed free of the hijacker and ran at the Widow. "Leave us alone!"

Herron struggled against his restraints as Lynda rained blows on the pirate leader. The Widow was forced back a step as she shifted her focus to defend herself, but once the element of surprise was gone, she quickly gained the upper hand. She took two more ineffectual punches before slapping away a third blow and gripping the young woman by the throat.

"I should flay you alive." She grinned as she squeezed tighter, then fixed her gaze on her henchman who'd let Lynda escape. "Or you."

"The last number is one!" Herron shouted, forcing the attention of the hijackers back to him. "Seven, Four, One, One."

"See, that wasn't so hard, was it?" The Widow gloated. "If the code is right, you'll die, but she'll live."

One hand still tight on Lynda's neck, she pointed at her humiliated associate and then the safe. The henchman nodded and bent down to enter the combination. And as he entered the last number, Herron closed his eyes.

There was a boom and, a second later, flames engulfed the wheelhouse as Herron's booby-trap was tripped, the wrong code setting it off. The explosion shattered the windows and threw the hijacker back, his face and torso horribly maimed. The Widow screamed, releasing Lynda as she instinctively covered her face from the heat.

Closer to the detonation, Herron felt like he'd been shoved into a furnace. He struggled to breathe, his lungs like they were filled with fire. "Fuck!"

"Fool!" The Widow hissed, backing out of the wheelhouse. With the safe destroyed and the yacht now useless, escape was her only option. "You could have had a quick death. Now you and your friend will burn or drown!"

Herron shouted curses at her as she slipped away, but a raging out-of-control inferno now engulfed the wheelhouse, so he only had a moment to act. The yacht was ablaze, and smoke was stealing the air—either fact could punch his departure ticket from the Earth—but his gambit had worked.

Triggering the trap had been their only chance to escape the boat; now they just had to pull it off.

He glanced at Lynda. Standing in the corner, she had been far enough from the explosion to escape injury, but she was obviously stunned, frozen in fear, her eyes locked on the blaze.

"Lynda!" His shout snapped her out of it. "Use the knife to free me!"

She blinked a few times, stared, and then ran over to him. She reached down to pick up the knife the dead hijacker had held to her throat, then got to work on the restraints. They were thick, so it took some time, all the while the pair of them inhaling black smoke from the blaze. Both were coughing by the time one hand was finally freed.

"Give me the knife!" Herron held out his free hand and took it. "Now go!"

She hesitated just a second, then nodded and ran for the door. The Widow might still be out there, but it was most likely she'd bailed, and the slight chance she'd stuck around was better than Lynda waiting for him and inhaling more smoke.

He'd already gambled with far worse odds and won.

He cut the restraints around his other wrist and then his ankles. He was stronger than Lynda, so he didn't take as long as her, although he coughed hard as smoke continued to fill his lungs. Free at last, he scampered around the wheelhouse to retrieve two lifejackets and an emergency beacon.

Nothing else was salvageable. The contents of his safe were ash. The price of saving their lives.

As he moved, he looked around for any sign of the Widow, but she was gone. Despite the fury she'd stoked in the pit of his stomach, rivalling the fire that was consuming his home, Herron had to let her go.

Lynda had her back pressed against the side rail of the yacht, staring at the blaze. "We have to save the boat..."

"Forget it." He shrugged, then quickly and roughly inspected her for any wounds or burns, then concluded she was fine. "We got lucky."

She didn't look convinced, but she nodded. "What do we do now? That woman took the other boat!"

Herron nodded. He'd expected that. But as he looked around the deck, he had a sinking feeling when he saw the yacht's self-inflating lifeboats were missing. The hijackers had clearly tossed them overboard to prevent anyone from escaping. It made things desperate for Herron and Lynda.

His back-up plan would have to do. "Strap up."

He helped Lynda into a lifejacket, then donned his own. After they were safely buckled in, he looked over his shoulder with wistful regret. By now, a third of the yacht was ablaze and the rest would soon follow. Herron watched his stricken home burn for just a second longer than necessary...

... then he gripped Lynda tight and took them both over the side.

* * *

HERRON GASPED as he plunged into the Pacific, the water icy compared to the heat in the wheelhouse. As his head went under, he struggled to breathe and swallowed a few mouthfuls of salt water, but he got over the shock and quickly broke the surface. After a momentary panic at being unable to see Lynda, she too popped above the water.

She coughed a few times, looking at him with wide eyes, as the pale light of the flames reflected off the surrounding water. "Mitch, I'm sorry..."

"It's just a boat." Herron lied. "I just need you to hang tough for a minute and then I'll get us out of here."

She nodded, and he led them in a swim around to the other side of the burning yacht. He didn't have far to go, but it was still a struggle given the punishment he'd taken from the Widow. They skirted the yacht and found the Zodiac boat that Smiley and the others who'd made it aboard had used...

It was a floating carcass, deflated rubber with bullet holes in it, with its engine nowhere in sight.

The Widow had been good to her word. She really had intended for them to burn alive on the yacht or drown when they escaped it. The boat was useless. He'd underestimated her. She was a formidable foe.

"Shit." Herron's voice was a whisper, because he didn't want to alert Lynda to the fact that the situation was desperate. He turned to smile at Lynda. "We're going to be okay."

"The other boat is gone, Mitch." Lynda saw the reality as clear as he did. "What are we going to do?"

Herron didn't have a simple answer. His first plan had been to use one of his own lifeboats to get them to safety. Second, to use whichever Zodiac the Widow hadn't taken. But his third was far more desperate, a plan that he found personally unsatisfactory but offered Lynda the best chance to survive.

Herron reached into his pocket and pulled out the nautical emergency beacon he'd taken from the wheelhouse. He popped off the plastic cover and his thumb hovered over the black button. As soon as he pressed it, a message would be sent that they needed help.

He felt ashamed for delaying for even a second, but he knew the second help arrived someone would piece it all together, figure out who he really was and arrest him. He'd be saving Lynda and condemning himself.

But he had no other choice.

He mashed the button.

The process was now in motion. They had no food or water, no way to dry themselves and no way to keep them warm. All they could do was wait, bobbing in the water, watching the carcass of his yacht be overcome by fire.

Seeing the boat burn, he felt regret. After he'd destroyed the Enclave and killed the Master, he'd been content with his nomadic life. But as the yacht succumbed, its husk slipping beneath the waves, he was unsure whether he'd been a fool to try hiding from his past.

Like it or not, he'd be back in the spotlight soon enough.

The yacht had long vanished under the sea, and Herron was growing ever more impatient for help to arrive. A few times, Lynda tried to speak with him, but he gave only the most basic responses. She soon got the point—understood his loss—and they had settled into silence—wet, cold, and powerless.

Eventually, he spotted the grey speck far off in the distance—a helicopter. Soon there was the *thump-thump-thump* drumbeat of rotors overhead and the United States Navy chopper was doing a long and lazy loop around them.

At last, it took up a position hovering near the Zodiac, and a sailor descended on a cable into the water. "Need some help?"

"You could say that," Herron replied.

"Are either of you wounded?"

"Cuts and bruises."

The sailor nodded and the rescue operation proceeded with all the usual efficiency of the United States forces. The sailor secured Lynda in a harness and winched her aboard the chopper first. A few minutes later, he returned and did the same for Herron. Neither man spoke—even if the roar of the rotor blades didn't prevent chat, the sailor too focused on his work.

Herron had nothing to say, anyway.

He'd never expected to ride in a U.S. military transport chopper again. His entire career in the special forces had involved being flown in and out of remote places, tasked with completing the most tough missions. But he'd never felt such a sense of dread as he did now, because at any moment he'd be exposed and there was no way to avoid it. On top of the loss of his yacht, losing his false identity would herald a new beginning for Herron.

A forced rebirth.

Perhaps noticing the look of unease on his face, the sailor who'd rescued them tapped Herron's arm and opened his headset comms. "What happened?"

"We were attacked by pirates." Herron paused, because everything else was a lie. "They took our valuables then torched the boat."

The sailor sighed. "If you'd sounded the alert earlier, we might have been able to save you from too much trouble."

"It all happened so fast..." Herron could hardly say that he'd fought off almost all the pirates himself. "What's the U.S. Navy doing this far out of the way?"

If the sailor noticed the change of topic, he didn't mention it. "We've been on patrol in these waters for months—it's a multinational effort to police piracy— but we're spread pretty thin."

"You were close enough to help us out." Herron forced a smile. "So that'll do me for the time being."

"You'll both be fine." The sailor grinned. "Good old Uncle Sam will make sure you're well taken care of."

Herron's nod masked his thoughts.

That's what I'm worried about.

2

Herron had been out of the military for a decade—since he'd turned his back on the special forces and been enlisted by the Enclave—yet riding in the chopper felt like coming home. The canvas seat like sandpaper on his skin, the safety harness that didn't fit quite right, the uniformed men seated across from him...

Dampened as it was by his headset, the constant thunder of the rotors was like a drumroll marking the end of this act of Herron's life. He sat in silence, occasionally glancing at Lynda—who seemed relieved and relaxed after their near miss——and used the time to ready himself for what was to come.

Because he was sure conflict was on the way.

The voice of the sailor who'd rescued them filled Herron's headset. "You're both going to be just fine!"

Herron gave him a thumbs up, because his false identity would last even less time if he looked unhappy about being rescued. "I appreciate you helping us!"

"Anytime, pal." The sailor smiled. "What's your name, anyway?"

"Dave Walsh." Herron gave the name of one of his many false identities now at the bottom of the ocean. "Are we almost there?"

The sailor nodded and, a minute later, the pilot reported over comms that they were close to landing. Herron looked out the windows of the chopper until he spotted a speck off in the distance—most likely an Arleigh Burke class destroyer, the setting for the next chapter of this strange day.

The chopper arced wide around the destroyer before hovering above the rear helipad. Already on the deck, near to another helicopter, Herron could see a welcoming party of a handful of sailors. That alone didn't trigger any alarm bells, but one other detail about the group sure as hell did.

Their assault rifles.

Herron kept as still as the dead while the chopper landed and powered down. The clatter of the rotors was replaced by the chatter of the crew, and he watched closely as one sailor climbed out of the chopper, then helped Lynda down onto the deck. He moved to follow.

"Not so fast, Mr Walsh." The sailor who'd rescued them clamped a hand on his shoulder. His earlier cheer had been replaced by a steely expression. "Captain wants you in the officers' wardroom."

Herron's muscles tensed instinctively, ready to explode with violence... but first he had to resolve this peacefully, for Lynda's sake. "I want to go with her."

"Your friend will be fine." The sailor kept his hand on Herron's shoulder. "You're going for a debrief."

Herron stared at him for a few seconds, but the

meaning was clear, and the navy man would not back down. Keeping their heads low as they moved out of the rotor's arc, he followed the sailor off the pad and towards Lynda.

"End of the line for our partnership, Lynda." Herron tried to force a smile, but he doubted it was convincing. "Go with these sailors. They'll take care of you from here and see you safely back to Fiji."

Her face was ashen, as if she'd only just realized they might be separated. "I stowed away so I could go with *you*, Mitch."

"That's not an option anymore." He waited while the reality sank in, then didn't back away when she sobbed and stepped forward to hug him. He wrapped his arms awkwardly around her. "It'll be okay."

"I'm sorry." She pressed her head against his chest. "If it wasn't for me, you wouldn't have used the beacon and put yourself in danger."

"You're wrong." Herron lied. She was a perceptive kid. "Go home, go to school and do something great with your life."

She pulled away and smiled at him, clearly upset but trying to put a brave face on it, just like she had when they'd threatened her on the yacht. "You'll come visit me in Fiji, won't you? Mitch?"

Herron winced inwardly at her use of his real name —a quick glance at the nearby sailor showed that he'd caught the mistake—and then he nodded, although he knew he'd never see her again. She was whisked away by the unarmed sailors, his own path blocked by a pair of sailors armed with assault rifles.

Herron fronted up to the sailors. Their weapons were pointed at the deck, but their bodies were stiff and their faces hard, which was enough to show him where he stood. "Am I being arrested?"

"You're being debriefed, but you can call it whatever you like." One sailor replied, his voice hard. "Come with us voluntarily or we'll drag you. Makes no difference to me."

There was no point arguing—yet. Normally he'd fight or run or hide in the shadows, but that was useless on a U.S. Navy destroyer in the middle of the ocean. He'd known the second he hit the emergency distress beacon that his old life of quiet and seclusion was over —if it had ever been real to start with—and now there was nothing he could do to stop it.

Herron took a deep breath and looked around. In the faces of the sailors guarding him, he saw a bunch of children, junior ranks who were oblivious to the horrors of the battlefield. They weren't part of some grand plot to bust him and deliver him stateside, at least not yet, rather regular sailors tasked to help civilians only to find one they weren't sure about.

As if to illustrate the point, a medic stepped away from the welcoming party and moved across to him. She couldn't be more than mid-twenties, fresh to the service. "Try to relax, you're in good hands."

"Sorry, I'm just on edge after the hijacking." Herron spoke slowly. "I'm not used to seeing so many guns."

"Understandable." Her voice was kind and concerned. "Come with me. I'll take care of your cuts and bruises while you wait for the captain...."

There was no other choice but to follow her off the deck and into his new life.

* * *

HERRON WINCED as the medic applied antiseptic to a laceration down his left cheek, one of the many injuries on his face. "That hurts more than the cut did."

"Then you should avoid getting cut." She gave him an impish grin. "Anyway, I'm done with you now."

"Glad to hear it." He waited for her to take a step back, although not very far in the tiny cell he was in. "How's Lynda doing?"

"The woman you arrived with?" The medic raised an eyebrow as she removed her latex gloves and pocketed them. "She's fine now she's dry and warm."

"Okay." Herron didn't press the issue with her—she was a just a junior sailor doing her job—instead he'd hold his fire until the captain showed up. "Thanks."

When she departed his cell at last, they left a guard outside the door. He hadn't been left alone at any point, the sailors clearly keen to understand who they had in their midst before he was given any freedom.

That thought depressed him. Because if he was under such close guard now, how would the sailors react when they inevitably cracked the veneer of his false identity? His fake credentials were good, but would they stand up to a determined interrogation by an already suspicious crew?

One call to the CIA or the FBI, plus a bit of time, would probably be enough.

Still, if he had to wait around for the captain to show, he'd done it in worse places. He'd spent days laying prone in the mud—staring down a rifle scope, pissing and shitting in place, and getting no sleep—so waiting on a bed in a climate-controlled cell was easy.

An hour later, Herron almost choked when the captain walked through the door, limping heavily, but otherwise projecting authority. "You've got to be kidding me..."

"Walsh?" The new arrival, a tall and muscular man, grinned down at Herron. "Who the hell is Walsh?"

Any hope Herron's false identity would hold up was detonated instantly. He sat up in the bed. "Laidlaw. Didn't expect to see you here."

Captain Jerome Laidlaw laughed. "I'm not sure if I should shake your hand, arrest you or shoot you."

Herron stood, reached out and shook Laidlaw's hand. "Given where we left things in Sinaloa, I'd put good money on the latter."

Laidlaw limped over to Herron and slapped him on the shoulder a few times. "It's really damn good to see you again, Mitch."

"Bullshit." Herron scoffed. "You've got the most wanted man on the planet aboard your ship. There's no way you're *happy* about it."

Laidlaw limped from the cell and returned a second later with a bottle of tequila and two glasses. He poured a hefty dose in each, then slid one to Herron. "Didn't have any ice, so this will have to do."

"Been a while." Herron held his glass up in a makeshift salute, then took a sip of the drink. It burned and instantly reminded him of the last time he'd had it. "You owed me a bottle."

Laidlaw grinned and took a sip of his own. "I haven't forgotten. In fact, I developed a bit of a taste for it."

The drink gave Herron a flashback to that time as well, serving with Laidlaw off the coast of Sinaloa, Mexico. Herron had been in charge of a small special forces unit charged with interdicting the supply of illegal narcotics into the United States, while Laidlaw had been in charge of the ship ferrying them around the coast.

The mission had gone for six months. It had been bloody work, with no quarter asked or given, a battle to the death against a cartel with billions of reasons to fight back. In months, Herron's team had blown up a half-dozen manufacturing facilities and warehouses, destroyed several aircraft used to fly supply over the border, and assassinated over twenty high-value targets.

Eventually, the cartel had stopped trying to defend itself and fought back. Unable to find Herron's team in the field, they'd instead targeted Laidlaw's ship after a leak in the Mexican military had revealed its location. The ship had been attacked while in port to re-supply, several of the crew killed and many wounded, and Laidlaw had been shot in the leg.

Then Herron's team had arrived.

Fresh from shove leave, the special forces squad had been low on sobriety but high on enthusiasm. They'd helped the sailors defending the ship to turn the tables. Herron himself had put down the sicario who'd been preparing to hold Laidlaw hostage to extract concessions from the U.S. government.

A bottle of tequila smashed over the killer's head had ended that threat.

In the aftermath, the mission had been ended, the Pentagon declaring mission accomplished and not willing to risk further attacks. Herron had been moved on to other missions, Laidlaw had healed and then been given command of another vessel, and the two of them had never got to taste the brand of tequila in the bottle he'd smashed over the Mexican's head.

Until now.

They spoke deep into the night, Laidlaw summarising his career since Herron had last seen him —long, distinguished, faultless. He had no family, a navy man who lived for the job and had been rewarded with command of a destroyer, one of the youngest captains to ever notch that achievement and with plenty more to come. He still had the limp, but otherwise the attack in Sinaloa hadn't impacted his career.

"What about you, Mitch?" Laidlaw's voice suddenly took a serious tone. "I don't buy this bullshit about you sailing the seven seas on your yacht."

Herron briefly weighed-up whether he should tell Laidlaw the truth. If his name was fed into a computer all would be revealed anyway, but it was more than that. Did their shared history and the fact Laidlaw hadn't already called in his identity mean he could trust his old comrade?

"When I left the military, I became a contract killer for a black-ops agency that purported to work for the US government." Herron crossed his arms across his chest as Laidlaw listened in stone-faced silence. "They deceived me, so I destroyed them. Now every intelligence agency on Earth wants me dead."

"That mess in London..." Laidlaw finally spoke. "I did wonder why you'd go to such lengths to put yourself on Interpol and the FBI's shit list."

"Now you know." Herron took a sip of his drink, his eyes never leaving Laidlaw. "So, what are you going to do?"

"I'm not going to expose you." Laidlaw laughed and then scratched his chin, like he was properly considering an idea he'd only toyed with previously. "We might be able to help each other out."

"Go on."

"I have a problem your unique blend of conflict resolution might help with. In return for keeping your presence here hidden."

"And the crew will go for it?"

"Sure, if it gets them home faster." Laidlaw shrugged. "They've been stuck out here for months, away from families and friends, watching paint dry."

"What's the issue?"

"Like always, they have not given us enough resources to do the job properly." Laidlaw scoffed. "Right now, we've been assigned three ships to cover half an ocean."

It was a common problem. The generals and bean counters were happy to overwhelm a traditional enemy on the field of battle, but less intense problems—like asymmetric conflict against a crude group of pirates—got cents in the dollar applied to them.

"The lack of resources makes our job impossible." Laidlaw continued as he poured himself another glass of tequila and topped up Herron's. "We're told to stop the hijackings, but the best I can do is send choppers to the ships they hit."

"The locals can't handle it?"

Laidlaw sighed. "The President of the Philippines denies the piracy is based out of his country and refuses to lift a finger to do anything to help stop it. 'Why not the CIA or the special forces?' will be your next question, but..."

"But the current *American* President is sensitive to claims of western imperialism in a former territory, so he's refusing to do anything more than police international waters."

Laidlaw grinned. "You *do* still read the news."

"Why not just launch a Tomahawk at their base?"

"Because bombing poor towns and villages doesn't go over well in the press." Laidlaw sipped his drink. "Not that it matters, I don't know even where the base is."

"The Vietnam Paradox." Herron let the words hang heavy in the air. "How do you remove a cancer from otherwise healthy tissue?"

"You use a damn sharp scalpel."

Herron leaned forward on his elbows. "I'm out of the business."

"And helping me will keep you out of it." The meaning in the captain's words was clear. "What do you think?"

Herron drained his whiskey. He could understand Laidlaw's need and why he was asking, but it still felt like blackmail. But in the captain's position, Herron might have done the same. "All right."

"That's what I wanted to hear." Laidlaw finished his own drink. "You're still spending the night in the brig, though."

Herron tensed. "Why the hell would I do that?"

Laidlaw frowned in confusion, then relaxed. "You really are paranoid, just like always. I need to keep you hidden. The more people see you on board, the harder it is not to report you being here."

"And I don't want to do that." Herron laid back down on the bed and closed his eyes, satisfied with the bargain he'd made, even though he knew it was blackmail. "I never knew you cared so much."

"I suggest you get some rest." Laidlaw stood,

gathered the glasses, and headed for the door. "Because it might be a while before you next can."

* * *

SOME HOURS LATER, Herron opened his eyes to the sound of a cough. Laidlaw stood in the doorway with a pair of duffel bags.

"Hope you got some sleep." The captain's voice was deadpan as he dropped the bags by Herron's bed. "Meet me outside when you're ready."

Laidlaw left as Herron rubbed his face and sat up. He bent down and examined the bags. One was filled with water, provisions, clothes, and footwear; the other held a combat knife, a suppressed submachine gun, a suppressed pistol, spare magazines, and a Manila folder filled with printed-out reports and photographs.

He got to work on the small stack of intelligence reports—it was as close to a mission brief as he was going to get, everything the Navy had on the pirates and the series of villages in eastern Philippines they were believed to operate from.

It seemed they had been sitting on intel about one member of the hijacking ring for a while—Herron was to go to his home and start working his way up the food chain. He studied the photographs and satellite imagery of the man's hometown, then moved on to the rest of the pack. It was general intelligence about the hijackers, their targets, and their tactics. There wasn't a lot, but it gave him a better idea about the group than he'd had before: they'd terrorised twenty-seven vessels in one year, dressing up their attacks as a statement against wealthy oppressors.

Their tactics were aggressive and, except for Herron and Lynda, they'd left nobody left alive on the ships they'd attacked. They struck, killed everyone, took what they could and then melted away before help could arrive.

A few times, he stopped to eat or take a swig from his canteen—when he was eventually done with the intelligence dossier, he burned it all with a Zippo lighter Laidlaw had included in the duffel bag. By the time the files were nothing but ash, he was prepared to set out, far more informed than before.

Now he knew the pirate's motivation: profit, above all else, but with enough of a veneer of anti-imperialism to allow them to hide among the locals.

He knew their victim profile: soft targets that belonged only to western countries—yachts and cargo ships with small crews that could be easily overwhelmed.

He knew their methods: shock and awe, overwhelming crews with waves of attackers, until they could ransack the vessel.

He knew the villages American intelligence suspected housed them: none were far inland, the nearest close enough for Herron to reach on foot within a day.

But, best of all, he knew where to start.

He dressed in the tactical gear, stuffed the remaining equipment into the bag and left the brig. Laidlaw was waiting outside and led him through the ship. The crew members they came across didn't make eye contact and, as far as they were concerned, he didn't exist.

He was a phantom.

Herron wasn't surprised. Since 9/11, servicepeople in all branches of the military were used to being in proximity to covert operations. Here, their captain had ordered them to ignore anyone unusual aboard their ship, so they did.

Eventually, they reached the rear of the ship, where the rescue helicopter waited in silence and darkness. Herron's first thought was that he'd be flying out to complete his mission, but Laidlaw moved past it and continued to the stern, where a pirate Zodiac waited, ready to be winched down to the water.

"We retrieved it after a previous attack." Laidlaw answered the unasked question. "We even hosed out the blood."

"Okay. Just point me in the right direction and I'll get moving."

"We're off the coast of the Philippines and as far as my men are concerned, Operation Azure Backlash is an official job well above their pay grade."

"So, no help there then."

"You'll have the area of operations to yourself, because nobody else will lift a finger to stop this problem." Laidlaw clamped a hand down on Herron's shoulder. "It's all up to you now."

"How aggressive you want me to be with these guys?"

"They're animals who prey on the vulnerable." Laidlaw stared out into the dark, unseeing. "I want them eradicated."

Herron nodded and then saluted Laidlaw. Despite the blackmail, he was still glad he'd run into Laidlaw rather than some other captain. "I'll get the job done."

Laidlaw returned the salute. "Nobody aboard this ship will expose that you've been here. I can't promise anything more."

Without further delay, Herron tossed the bag into the boat and then climbed inside, then waited as the boat was lowered into the ocean. When it was in the water, he fired up the engine, checked his compass, and eased the Zodiac away from the destroyer and within a few minutes found himself alone.

He settled in for the long journey to land with only the soft buzz of the boat's engine for company, alone with his thoughts under the stars as he had so often been before, sailing the Pacific on his yacht. Would this be the last time, given he'd lost his home and been pulled back into his old life?

Was it even possible for a man like him to live in peace?

He contemplated the question as the boat chewed up the miles to shore, his mood lifting as the first ray of sunshine peered over the horizon. Within minutes, the sunrise was a welcoming beacon dead ahead of him and soon after, and the shore came into sight.

The boat cut through the waves, and Herron beached it on the sand. A quick look around showed there was no sign of anyone nearby. It was all surf, sand, and palm trees—paradise. Except Herron knew that, somewhere in the jungle, there was a big enough threat to cause the deployment of a United States Navy flotilla.

A big enough threat to drag him back into the life he'd sworn to leave behind.

After one last check to make sure nobody had spotted him, Herron hefted the duffel bag over his shoulder, climbed out of the boat and dragged it up onto the sand. It only took a minute to reach the treeline, at which point he pulled out his combat knife and went to work. With more gusto than necessary, he slashed the rubber inflatable in a dozen places, collapsing the boat.

He took a minute to hide the remains against the trunk of a tree and then cover it with foliage. Ideally, he'd bury it, but he didn't have the time or the tools for that. He had to get away from here fast in case he'd been spotted. Still, by the time he was done, he was satisfied someone would need to step right nearby to see the boat, which was good enough.

Leaving it behind. Herron disappeared into the trees.

3

_____

Herron ran a hand through his hair. It had been slowly receding over the past few years, but whatever he lacked, the day-long trek through the Philippine jungle on the way had replaced with sweat. That and, if he was being honest, too much inactivity on a boat.

Although he'd made a brief return to his old life to stop a civil war in Fiji, Herron felt his edge had dulled a little. He was a little older, a little slower. In Fiji, it hadn't mattered; here, he doubted it would either, but it made him wonder if he'd have what it took when faced with a genuine threat. One only the best could overcome.

Like a fellow assassin or a team of elite killers.

The thought still on his mind, Herron wiped his sweaty hand on his shorts and continued inland through some of the hardest terrain he'd yet encountered. It would have been easier to take the road towards the town, and he might have been able to hitch a ride, but that would have cost him the chance to scout his first objective—the home of the hijacker identified in the dossier.

He checked his compass to confirm he was still on the right path, then continued overland. Sweat continued to drip down his face, his hair and his clothes wet with perspiration. A few times, nasty-looking bugs landed on him, ready to take a bite—he smashed them into pulp with a quick slap.

Three miles out, he took a break. He wanted to wait until darkness before he entered the town, yet nightfall was still half-a-dozen hours away. He rested with his back against a tree, in the sort of half-awake slumber common on a mission. It was restful, but he was ready to explode into action if needed.

When sunset was near, he opened his eyes. With no great urgency, he ate his fill and sucked down some water, then he geared up and moved out. The last few miles were slower going than earlier because he was being more cautious, but he ran into no trouble.

Finally, he reached a small hill that overlooked the town. Under the pale moonlight and a pair of streetlamps, he could see two rows of ramshackle houses—around two dozen in total—separated by a dirt road down the middle. There were a few rusted white sedans and pickup trucks parked along the street, but otherwise the only other sign of modernity was a flashing Coca-Cola sign on the side of what looked like the general store.

He surveyed the settlement for twenty minutes, looking for any obvious defensive perimeter or armed guards, but failing to identify either. While he was sure at least one civilian in the town was involved in the pirate attacks, he did not know how far the cancer had spread. He might have to deal with a single criminal, or an entire town filled with them.

He set off slowly, careful not to step on any dry branches or trip on a rock. His footfalls as soft as a whisper, he approached the town perpendicular to the main road that ran down its centre and headed behind one row of houses. Few had lights on, and he could see no significant activity inside any of them.

He reached the rear of one of the illuminated houses and peered through a window. With lights on inside and darkness out, he could have been dressed in bright pink and still been invisible to anyone looking out, so he took his time seeing if anyone was home. Eventually, after a few moments, an older woman appeared in the living room and sat on a sofa, but there was no sign of his target.

He repeated the process a few more times with other houses, those inside oblivious to the fox casing their henhouse. None of those he saw matched the photograph of the hijacker, and he lost patience. He needed to change things up.

Careful to stay concealed, he moved along towards the general store with the neon Coke sign, which blazed like a sun on the dimly lit street. Here was the only real chance he'd get to quickly locate his target.

He broke from the darkness and walked beneath the Coke sign, risking exposure for only a second, then hugged the shadows out in front of the store again before surveying the interior. An elderly man was behind the counter. He looked frail, and Herron figured he had little time left.

That fact changed his plan of attack. In his old life, as a member of the Enclave, he would have set the store on fire as he'd originally planned; now, however, he wouldn't cause trouble for a guy who couldn't stand it.

He sighed. "You're too damn nice, Mitch..."

Herron looked around for a new target as he reached into his pocket and pulled out his Zippo lighter. He settled on the carcass of a rusted old sedan right out front of the store. Keeping low, he skulked towards it and crouched down near the driver's door. Sheltered from the street and confident the old shopkeeper wouldn't spot him, he went to work.

He tested the handle first and was pleased to find the rust bucket unlocked; better, the interior light failed to come on when the door was opened. Without delay, he set light to the soft interior features of the sedan— the fabric seat covers, carpets and floor mats—and then wound down the window. The job done, he closed the door and slinked away.

While the fire took some time to take hold, once it did it quickly consumed the fuel inside the vehicle. Soon, the fire had spread through the whole car and to the foam of the seats themselves. Next, as the temperature increased and the flames became more intense, the soft plastics burned as well. Within minutes, the whole car was an inferno.

All the while, Herron watched and waited.

The first call of alarm came from the elderly store owner, who rushed outside and shouted for help, then valiantly tried to douse the flames with a fire extinguisher. He achieved little, nor did the few dozen people who spilled out of the houses and came running to help, the entire town ill-equipped to put out the blazing vehicle.

But as everyone focused on the car, resigned to the fact that they'd failed to control the fire, Herron's attention was elsewhere. In the light of the fire and the Coke sign, he scanned the faces of all those who'd come to help. Almost at once, he spotted the man he was looking for.

It was time for a chat about the loss of his yacht.

HOURS LATER, once the town had settled back into slumber, Herron slid open a window of the hijacker's house. It raised up smoothly on its runners, and he was glad he wouldn't have to force the lock or break in. Silently, he climbed through, then closed the window behind him. Still as a corpse, he listened, alert for any sign that his intrusion had disturbed the occupants of the house.

After a minute, he was confident enough to move.

He stalked down the corridor and searched each room he passed. The bathroom, kitchen and small living room were empty, although the old television was turned on and muted. That left only the bedroom at the front of the house near the entrance. The door to the bedroom itself was closed, but it would be a mistake to assume the hijacker was asleep.

Herron drew his pistol and eased the door all the way open. The man was on his back in the bed, eyes closed. He was young, his bare chest visible—rising and falling slowly—and his lower body covered by a threadbare blanket.

He aimed the pistol at his sleeping target and

searched the room for weapons, checking the side table and dresser. Then, satisfied there was nothing within reach, he clamped a hand down on the man's mouth and pressed the barrel of the pistol against his skull.

The hijacker inhaled sharply through his nose and his eyes shot open.

Herron smiled down at him. In the darkness, dressed all in black, he figured he looked like death himself. Now he had the man's attention, he whispered. "Do you speak English?"

The man nodded quickly.

"Good." Herron flicked on the lamp and stepped away from him. "Lower the bedcovers slowly with your hands in my sight. If you do anything stupid, I'm going to put a bullet in your head."

The hijacker nodded and pushed down the bedsheets. Herron flicked his eyes between the man and the areas of the bed that were newly exposed, alert for any hidden weapon. But by the time the sheet was down near the foot of the bed, it was clear there were no nasty surprises. Satisfied, Herron took another step back, but kept the gun aimed at the kid.

"What's your name?"

"Carlos Bautista." The kid stammered the words, eyes locked on the pistol. "Why are you here?"

Herron gave a bitter laugh. "Someone hijacked my boat."

Bautista sighed. He understood now. "What do you want to know?"

"Where can I find your boss?"

Bautista shook his head. "You don't know what dealing with."

"So, tell me."

"I don't–"

Herron moved in and slapped him across his ear. "Talk."

"Okay!" Bautista sat up in the bed. "I don't know who is in charge. They send us a message with the target and starting location. We meet at the location, and our boats and weapons are already there."

"You know *nothing* ahead of time?" Herron raised an eyebrow. "Not the other hijackers? Times or dates?"

Bautista shook his head. "It's all done via WhatsApp. We meet at the boats, do the job, and then go our separate ways. I don't know anyone else, and they don't know me."

"But you're happy to steal with them..."

"I won't apologize for doing what I have to do to live." Bautista practically spat the words at him. "Things aren't exactly great around here."

"What do you do with the cash and the items you steal? FedEx them to whoever is coordinating the job?"

"One of us delivers it to the capital at a specific place and time that they message to us. I can't give you a location because they change all the time."

Herron sighed. A network so dispersed was hard to disrupt—you were always one step behind, and even if you squashed one target, another simply emerged. U.S. intelligence had dealt with that problem during the War on Terror, and it applied here equally. He couldn't hit one target or one location and declare the job a success. He'd have to do it the hard way.

Herron levelled the pistol at Bautista again. "I want your phone and the next piece of the puzzle—a name or location to get me off your ass and onto someone else's."

"The phone is in the pocket of my jeans. I have nothing else to give you. Everything is done through the phone."

Herron dug the handset out of the pants and tucked it away. With a lead to the next link in the chain secured, he had no further need for Bautista. In the past, he would have snipped off the loose end with no qualms— just another victim in a business they'd both chosen— but he'd sworn those times were behind him. Unfortunately, he couldn't see how to let the pirate live and keep his mission secret.

He let out a regretful sigh. "Close your eyes..."

The phone in Herron's pocket beeped.

"That's a job!" Bautista's voice was frantic, all his defiance gone as his eyes flicked from Herron to the pistol, moments from death. "A job!"

Herron kept his gaze and the pistol on Bautista. Was this some sort of trick or trap by a desperate man? He relented and pulled out the phone. The screen displayed a WhatsApp message in a language Herron didn't understand, but that potentially gave him a way out of his ethical dilemma.

He turned the phone towards Bautista. "Can you tell me the target?"

"Sure." The young hijacker's voice trailed off as he read the message. "It's a big one..."

* * *

HERRON KEPT the pistol jammed into Bautista's back as they waited at the edge of the treeline, where the forest met the beach. He probably needn't have bothered, because the pirate had done little to suggest he'd go rogue and risk a bullet, even as they'd driven in Bautista's car to the meeting point.

But Herron hadn't lived this long in his profession by being careless.

On the sand, three Zodiacs waited, just like the ones that had attacked his yacht. They looked pristine, like some deity had simply reached down and planted them on the shore. Bautista, meanwhile, was sticking to his story, reiterating that for each job he simply showed up to the coordinates he was given to find the boats and the other hijackers.

The only difference this time was Herron's presence.

"Nobody will approach the boats if they see us together." Bautista repeated himself for the third time. "You need to let me go if you want to join the raid."

"Horseshit. You already told me none of the hijackers know any others, so they're just going to think I'm Johnny Pirate to your Tony Pirate. No, you're not getting away that easy."

Bautista didn't respond, his chance gone to scurry away like a rat. Even though he had been a model citizen and given Herron no reason to shoot him, it was still possible his information about the raids was bullshit or that he knew more than he'd revealed.

Herron wouldn't let him out of his sight until he knew for sure.

Time passed and Herron grew ever more impatient for the other hijackers to arrive. A few times, cars drove along the road that separated the forest and the beach, but none of them was stopping to join a piracy attack in international waters.

Herron was just about ready to give up when at last a car pulled off the road and stopped. A man got out, pulling on a dark ski mask. He jabbed Bautista in the back with the pistol. "Do you know him?"

"No. We don't share personal information."

"Right." Herron lowered the weapon. "Then let's get our costumes on."

They put on the balaclavas Bautista had supplied, and now they looked the part. Herron gestured with his chin towards the boats. He let Bautista take the lead, keeping his hand around the pistol, now in the pocket of his tactical pants.

With his other hand, Herron greeted the new arrival, who was near the boats by now. The mystery hijacker reciprocated, which showed that they were friendly pirates, if nothing else. Soon enough, others appeared to join them: ten others, each of them male and masked.

Herron stood back as the group prepared for the operation. None of it was by command: the group seemed democratic and chaotic, but clearly worked well enough together to have had some success over the past few months.

No more.

Herron removed the pistol from his pocket... only to have Bautista grip his wrist.

Bautista kept his voice low. "You don't understand. If you take them out here, the mission won't go ahead..."

Herron jerked his hand away, the pistol with it, and pocketed the weapon. "You better tell me something good."

Bautista checked no one had noticed their

exchange, then leaned in close. "If the attack doesn't happen, the leadership will know. They'll schedule a shift change: our entire roster will be purged, and they'll go find some new people to attack the boats."

"Just like that?"

"The supply of men is plentiful, given the state of the economy. And it keeps the leaders protected."

"It's happened before?"

"I'm not sure. But they tell us that if one person fucks up, everyone is out of a job."

Herron thought about it, but only one thing didn't stack up. "How do they know the attack has happened?"

"When we're close to the objective, we send them a WhatsApp message and a photo of the target."

Herron kept quiet for a few moments, amending his plans on the fly. He'd originally hoped to take out this group before the attack, and then wait for the message to Bautista's phone informing him of the drop off for the loot. Then he'd just show up to take care of the leaders. But if Bautista spoke the truth, killing the hijackers now would sever Herron's connection to the paymasters.

None of the other hijackers had realized they'd been seconds from death. Their death might still come, but Bautista's intervention had won them the opportunity to breathe for another hour or two. It had also meant that for Herron to have a shot at wiping out the network, innocent sailors would have to be attacked.

It was brutal arithmetic for those men aboard the target ship but would serve the greater good.

With the matter decided, Herron helped the others finished their preparations. Each hijacker chose their own vessel to travel in, then the boats got on their way.

The buzz of the engines gave Herron flashbacks to the Zodiac swarm that had attacked his yacht, but he forced the images to the back of his mind.

To pull this off, he was going to need to focus.

4

Herron closed his eyes and sucked in the sea air as the Zodiac he shared with Bautista and two other hijackers inched ever closer to their destination. Ahead of them, barely visible in the inky blackness, two more Zodiacs also approached the target: a container ship outlined by white lights all along its hull.

The ship was enormous, so vast Herron's yacht would have looked like a child's toy next to it. An attack on such an enormous vessel by a dozen armed men in three small rubber boats seemed foolish, but Bautista had told him the container ship only had a small crew and was a prime target.

The contents of the ship would be a smorgasbord of loot for the hijackers, a menu so vast that it was almost impossible to comprehend. Yet the pirates had been ordered to ignore the contents of the hold and focus only on one small strongbox. Bautista had said such an order was uncommon—usually the job was to simply take whatever items of value they could find.

That piqued Herron's interest.

Whatever was inside that box, the pirate leadership had calculated it was worth a further escalation of the conflict. A yacht was one thing, but an attack on one of the giant, inviolable symbols of international trade would bring down a lot more heat. That seemed lost on the thieves doing the job, though.

"Almost there!" Bautista shouted to be heard over the buzz of the engine, his eyes locked on Herron. "Everybody cool?"

Herron nodded, but kept quiet. He was focused on the target vessel and the other Zodiacs in front of him. The collective drone of their engines made them sound like a swarm of locusts, which felt right, given the situation. Only Bautista knew Herron was here to control the pests.

As they neared the ship, Bautista and the others pulled out satellite phones and took photos, sending them over WhatsApp to confirm the attack was imminent. Herron waited until all the phones were back in their pockets and the attention of the hijackers was back on the job. Then he got to work.

"Wow!" Herron whistled, the sound masking his movement as he inched closer to the other hijackers. "Sure is big!"

In one explosive burst, Herron shoved the pilot of the boat overboard in a mess of limbs. The man screamed before he disappeared beneath the waves— alive and able to stay that way if he could swim. That small mercy, however, was enough to alert Bautista and the other hijacker that there was a problem.

Before either could react, Herron drew his pistol and aimed at them. While Bautista just stared, the remaining pirate tried to draw his own weapon. That mistake cost him the chance to jump overboard himself; Herron squeezed on the trigger twice, the shots hitting the man in the chest. He slumped to the floor of the boat.

Herron kept his weapon trained on Bautista as he removed the balaclava from his head. When it was off, he breathed deeply. "Well, now we have a problem."

"You told me if I led you to the target, you'd let me live…" Bautista's voice was panicked and desperate. "Please…"

"You will not die…" Herron grabbed the lifejacket at his feet and tossed it underarm to Bautista. "Put that on."

The young man made no move to take the buoyancy aid. "If you turn the boat around, we can head back to the beach and have no part of this…"

"I want to be part of this." Herron snarled, rapidly losing patience. "Last chance to save yourself."

"Okay." Bautista's shoulders slumped. He put on the lifejacket, tightened the straps, then paused. "You don't have to do this…"

"Bye." Herron shoved him overboard. Bautista screamed as he fell into the water, immediately left in the wake of the high-speed boat. "Asshole."

Herron turned his attention to the engine. He gripped the tiller, throttled up and adjusted his course slightly to head for the pair of Zodiacs ahead of him. He doubted the hijackers aboard them had heard the ruckus behind them, so he had a chance.

He tried to close in, catch up with them before they boarded the container ship, but he was too far behind. By the time he reached the massive hull, the other pirates were already aboard, and he heard the first gunshots pop off. Unable to dispose of the hijackers before reaching the target, he'd have to improvise now.

He sighed. "Never easy…"

Manoeuvring his Zodiac alongside one other, he grabbed one of the grappling ropes and started up the side of the ship, keen to get on deck and stop the imminent bloodshed. His muscles powered him on, inch by inch, until finally he pulled himself over the side with a grunt.

He drew his pistol and was surprised to see one of the other hijackers lying nearby in a pool of blood. He checked for a pulse, but the man was dead, a bullet wound to the head. Either he'd been betrayed by one of his own or Bautista had been wrong about the crew and there was a well-equipped security force aboard.

It made the mystery of what was inside that locked box even more interesting…

* * *

HERRON GRIPPED HIS PISTOL TIGHT, his back pressed against one of the ship's cargo containers, ears straining for any hint of what was around the corner: a tough gig over the wail of emergency sirens. When he heard nothing, he waited five seconds, inhaled sharply and then stepped out. As he moved, he scanned for any targets up ahead, but all he could see were more containers and more long stretches with no cover.

It was a problem he hadn't expected when he'd boarded the ship. End-to-end, the vessel was gigantic. Walking the length of the deck on his way to the bridge was like Groundhog Day. Each row of containers was followed by countless others, different colours and with different logos, but otherwise the same. As he'd advanced, careful and calculated, he'd spotted a hundred potential points of ambush—blind spots created by containers, ladders and ramps that led above-and-below decks, small rooms, and offices.

With no choice but to hurry to the business end of the ship, where the hijackers would be headed, Herron had scanned for threats as best he could but not as thoroughly as he'd like. Yet no danger had materialised. From the sounds of gunshots that chattered sporadically ahead of him, the ship's security had retreated to hold the bridge, leaving the way clear for him.

He had just thought he might make it to the bridge unscathed, when an alarmed shout caused him to tense.

"Shit." His eyes shot to the right, and he saw two uniformed security guards going for their weapons. Quickly, he held up one hand as his other reached for his pistol. "Guys, wait—"

Ignoring his plea, the guards immediately opened fire with their pistols, sharp cracks over the cacophony of the sirens. Herron dived for cover as bullets bored into containers and ricocheted off the metal guard rails around him. None hit him, but he was pinned down with no easy options. He wouldn't kill these guards. They were just men just doing their jobs.

"*Think*, Mitch." Herron chided himself. There'd be nothing left to save if he didn't deal with these guys quickly and get to the bridge. "*Think*."

More shots pounded into the side of the container he sheltered behind. Calm but desperate, he looked around for anything that might help him turn the tables. But even with the deck brightly lit by overhead halogens and the red emergency lights, he could see nothing obvious.

Except the lights themselves.

Herron aimed and fired several times. Each shot took out a globe and made the deck just a little darker. His weapon was silenced, but the showering glass and increasing shadows soon alerted the guards to his actions. Their fire slackened in response; no doubt they were too focused on cover to effectively return fire.

When he'd taken out all the lights he could see from cover, Herron peeked around the corner and took out the largest lights in the no-man's-land between him and the guards. One, two, three, four: the long overhead halogens mounted on lamp-poles went out, and in seconds, there was darkness enough to give him a chance of escape.

Herron reloaded and emerged from cover. He ran along the length of the container until he was on the walkway on the far side of the deck. If the lights had been intact, the guards would have been able to spot him instantly, but with only a few red emergency lights to brighten the inky darkness, the black-clad Herron could sneak past.

He moved past one container...

Two...

A pistol pressed into the side of his head.

"Move one more inch I'll blow your brains out. Drop the gun."

Herron did so. "Okay, just relax for a second..."

"Thought you could sneak away?" The guard scoffed and kicked the pistol across the deck. "Well, we've got you bottled up tight, and your buddies are next."

"You win." Herron slipped into the role of a hijacker, a criminal who realized the game was up. "Please don't hurt me."

"Like your friends hurt my pal?" The guard's voice was full of pain. "Pushed him overboard as soon as they boarded. He was having a smoke at the other end of the ship and now he's gone."

Herron kept quiet.

"You're lucky I'm not a murderer, you asshole. But bet your ass I'm going to see you put behind bars." He shoved Herron. "Start walking."

Herron nodded and moved in the direction the guard had specified, closer to the bridge, where the lights hadn't been shot out. He tried to play the part of a defeated foe, even as another guard joined them.

As the additional guard approached, handcuffs ready to slap on his wrists, Herron murmured, "Sorry, guys."

Gripping the wrist of the guard with the pistol—who'd relaxed just a second too early—Herron twisted until the weapon fell to the deck. He scooped it up and aimed it at the stunned guards.

"Be smart." He took a step back, maintaining his aim at the guards, who were smart enough to freeze. "You both have cuffs?"

They nodded.

Herron kept his voice calm and professional. "I want both of you to cuff your wrists to the safety railing and then toss the keys to me. But do it quick because I need to go save your captain."

The men were confused, but they still had a pistol pointed at them, so they complied. In unison, they locked one arm of the handcuffs around a wrist and then secured the other arm to the rail, just as Herron had asked. When they were done, they tossed their keys at his feet.

Herron kept his pistol and his eyes on them as he picked up the keys and tossed them overboard. "I'm going to check the cuffs are secure. If they're not, I'm going to shoot you. Want to check before I do?"

One guard shook his head, but the other—the man who'd first ambushed Herron—let out a lengthy sigh and tightened his cuffs until they locked around the rail with a click. Clearly, he hadn't given up on the idea of being a hero, but the threat of death had made him think again.

The two guards were out of the fight, and Herron was back in it. And on his way to the bridge.

* * *

THE BRIDGE SAT high above the containers, with large glass windows letting the crew see far and wide. There were two doors that granted entry, upstairs from the left and right side of the deck. Herron assumed there was a third inside that ran from the crew quarters.

Already, the bridge was under siege, guards inside firing through broken windows at the hijackers below. The pirates returned fire from behind containers, some on the left, some on the right, their torrent of bullets threatening to overwhelm the defenders. It was a stalemate, but Herron didn't see how the beleaguered crew could hold out for long.

Not without help, anyway.

He charged forward and joined the hijackers behind cover near the left side staircase. "Sorry. Got held up..."

"There's two guards giving us hell." One of the other pirates looked around at Herron. He hesitated, taken aback by Herron's exposed face. His exposed *white* face. "Lose your balaclava?"

"Something like that." Herron aimed his pistol at the hijacker and cleared his throat. "There's been a change of plans."

The rest of the group turned to face him, and Herron was suddenly amused at his inability to see the confusion on their faces—they still wore their balaclavas. A second later, the first of them tried to aim a weapon at Herron, so he shot the guy in the knee. He dropped to the ground, writhing.

"The next person who tries anything gets one too." Herron smiled. "Now, I want one of you to wrap something tight around his leg while the rest of you use zip ties to restrain your neighbour."

The shouts of outrage began. The threats washed over him, because this whole band was about as hard as puppy shit—a collective of two-bit crims banded together to prey on vulnerable civilians. Herron could understand their resistance, but he couldn't abide it.

He aimed at the apparent ringleader and took out his knee as well. As he fell, the others fell into line. As ordered, they dressed the wounds of the two kneecapped men, then used their own zip ties on each other—equipment that would otherwise have been used on the bridge crew.

When the job was done, four men were restrained on the deck, two of them with bullet wounds.

The attack on the bridge from the left thwarted, Herron was tempted to try the same on the right. But when several shots from the remaining hijackers pounded into the container he was sheltered behind, the decision was made for him. He popped up and fired at the hijackers, missing them all but forcing them to seek more cover.

It showed the crew on the bridge that he was a friend.

He hoped that was enough to keep him alive as he broke into a run, racing up the stairs. Each footfall clanged loudly, each step taking an eternity, but the bridge crew held their fire. He made it most of the way to the top, just three steps away, when a pair of hijackers popped up and opened fire on him.

"Shit!" Shots ricocheted off the steel steps and guard rails, which drowned out the sound of Herron hammering on the door of the bridge. "Let me in!"

His shots at the pirates, combined with the fact that the hijackers had fired at *him*, convinced the crew to help. The door was unlocked and opened, and Herron dived inside and to the ground to escape the gunfire.

Looking up, he saw one guard aiming a gun at him while another fired out at the hijackers. Herron grinned. "Hi guys, I'm Mitch. I'm here to help."

As the guard kept the pistol trained on him, a third man stepped forward and stood over Herron. The captain. "You're the newest addition to a very confusing situation. Explain yourself."

Herron sat up but made no move to stand in case the guard had an itchy trigger finger. "I'm working undercover for the U.S. Government. I'm here to stop the raids on shipping."

The captain scoffed. "Funny way of showing it."

Herron fixed him with a hard gaze. "You can either

accept my help and the chance I can get you out of this mess..."

The captain's eyes narrowed. "Or?"

"Or you detain me in the few moments you have before your boat, your cargo, your life and the lives of your crew are taken from you."

As if to illustrate the choice, the guard near the window screamed and clutched his shoulder, blood oozing between his fingers. The captain had a split second to choose: trust Herron enough to peel his other security guy off and fight the hijackers, or keep Herron under guard while the hijackers storm up the stairs and waltz through the door.

Herron held his gaze. "I can help you push them back, but you've got two seconds to decide."

The captain eyed him stonily, then nodded. "Okay."

Herron climbed to his feet as his custodian ran over to take the place of the wounded man, opening fire at the hijackers as they started up the stairs. Herron grabbed the injured guard's pistol from the deck and joined in.

They caught the attackers in the no-man's-land between the bridge and their cover.

One was shot in the leg. He screamed in pain and fell to the ground.

Another took two shots, one in the gut and one in the throat.

The last Herron drilled between the eyes.

Silence descended over the ship, broken only by the heavy sighs of relief from everyone left on the bridge— the captain, the guard who was still on his feet, and a pair of other unarmed crewmen. The wounded guard had passed out, but all four of the conscious crewmen were clearly stunned. They'd soon be in shock and would bear the scars of the attack for years.

Herron felt guilty that he'd let the attack go ahead at all, but it had been necessary to keep his only chance of climbing to the top of the pirate organisation's power structure. Now, he owed it to the dead men to finish the job.

The captain clamped a fleshy hand down on his shoulder. "I appreciate you helping me to deal with those men. But what do we do now?"

"Well, I'd start by freeing the two guards I cuffed to the guard railing about halfway along the deck. As for the hijackers, do whatever you like with their bodies..."

"We've got a freezer section. We can put them on ice until we reach port. We'll radio ahead to tell them that—"

Herron interrupted. "I need you to keep the attack quiet for a few days. Doing so will help dozens of other captains on dozens of other ships..."

The captain hesitated. "If I'm to understand you correctly, you're telling me the problem is being dealt with?"

Herron nodded. "Two days."

"What are you, CIA?" The captain raised an eyebrow when Herron didn't respond. "I understand. You've got 48 hours before I report the attack. I'll blame a broken radio."

"Thank you. It will help to put these guys out of business for good."

"I hope you have more success than those navy boys. We sure were happy when they got put on the beat, but they haven't done a damn thing." The captain scoffed. "Is that all you need from us?"

"Not quite." Herron let the words hang for a moment. "The gang wanted to crack open a strongbox and steal the contents. I need to look inside. I've got the code."

"You could ask to sleep with my wife and I might even consider it right now." The captain laughed. "Follow me."

5

———

Herron whistled a tune as he walked down the aisle of the small dollar store, plastic basket in hand. He'd packed it with all sorts of junk, but he wasn't done yet. He still had two more large duffel bags to fill, so he kept pulling bulky stuff off the shelves and adding to his haul. The entire time, he could feel eyes on him—the shopkeeper behind the counter, confused by this strange shopping spree.

After he'd departed the container ship, Herron had taken one of the Zodiac boats back to the shore. As soon as he'd been back in cell range, he'd used Bautista's phone to send a message to the only pre-saved number in its address book—lying that he had the loot from the strongbox and needed drop orders.

Then, while he'd waited for the orders to come in, he'd got to work trying to replicate the gold and platinum bars he'd found stored in the ship's strongbox.

With his fourth basket filled, he walked to the counter, put it on top, grabbed another basket and kept on going. As he did, the store owner continued to tally the cost of his purchases, stuffing the goods into the large duffel bags Herron had provided. Already they were heavy with crap he had bought.

Herron repeated the process until the shopkeeper had filled a half-dozen duffel bags with many baskets full of junk. When the bags were as full as they could be, he zipped them all closed. A quick check confirmed they were heavy enough to pass for fake bars of precious metal. It was the best he could do at short notice.

He put a wad of cash on the counter and raised an eyebrow. "Good?"

"Yes." The shopkeeper spoke passable English. "No change."

Herron laughed at the gall of the man, but agreed. It didn't matter. The shopkeeper was happy with the haul and Herron was happy to burn some cash to take the next step along the path to the hijacker leadership.

As if on cue, the phone in his pocket beeped.

He pulled out the handset, looked at the message, and frowned. He couldn't understand it, so he held the screen up to the shopkeeper. "Can you read this?"

The man looked down at the phone. "Sure. It's an address about fifteen minutes from here. Do you need directions?"

"I'll punch it into the maps application." Herron wrote the address in English and then pocketed the phone. "*Now* you can keep the change."

With the shopkeeper still chuckling, Herron hefted a pair of the duffel bags and left the dollar store. The man followed with two more. Herron popped the trunk of Bautista's car and stuffed the bags inside while the store owner went back inside for the last pair.

With a last nod at the owner, Herron slammed the trunk closed and rounded to the driver's side. He opened the door, climbed inside the car, gunned the engine, and hit the road. Maybe it was his imagination, but the back of the car felt heavier, weighed down by the bags of junk.

With that idle thought still strong in his mind, he ordered the virtual assistant on the phone to pull up directions to the rendezvous. The device promptly displayed a map to the drop-off point, with an estimated drive time of fifteen minutes, a full forty-five earlier he needed to be there.

He kept the car going a few miles per hour slower than the speed limit, eager to avoid any attention from overzealous local law enforcement. Fifteen minutes later—right on time—he pulled his car down a quiet-looking side street. A handful of children played outside a handful of houses and beyond them stood a few small warehouses with signs Herron couldn't read.

He slowed the car, his eyes darting between the phone and the properties he passed as he tried to figure out the exact rendezvous point. Then he found it: a secluded lane between two warehouses, little more than a dirt road, sunk in shadow from the monoliths on either side of it.

Herron cruised past. To any observer, he'd be just a white guy in a beaten-up car, out of place but unremarkable, with nothing to suggest he was the bagman for a network of international thieves. If the lane was under surveillance—and if he oversaw the drop-off and pickup, it would be—he hoped he'd avoided attention of any watchers.

He used the time he had up his sleeve to drive past

another couple of times, but the story was the same—a quiet alleyway in a quiet street, the playing kids the only sign of activity. After the third lap, he was satisfied he'd done what he could to spot any observers.

He parked thirty yards from the alleyway, killed the engine, and checked his watch. Thirty-five minutes until the pickup. He settled in, using five minutes to suck down some supplies he'd purchased from the dollar store—a bottle of water and some snack food.

With thirty minutes to go before the pickup, the street seemed normal. But still the hairs on the back of Herron's neck stood on end, telling him there was danger close by and that he should be cautious. It was an instinct that had served him well over the years, so as he drained the last of the water, he scanned the area for a way to deal with any potential threat.

He locked eyes on the group of kids and smiled.

* * *

It was amazing what twenty bucks could still buy you.

As Herron watched the kids haul the junk to the drop-off—two to a bag—he checked up ahead, then used the mirrors to scan the street behind him, knowing the hijackers could show up at any moment. There were still twenty minutes to go before the scheduled pickup, but Herron did not know if the crew was punctual.

Nobody had arrived by the time the kids were done. When they returned, he held a hand through the window with their cash in it. One of the kids snatched away. The boy—the oldest in the group—gave a conspiratorial grin, then set off back towards his house, his younger peers on his heels. Herron paid them no more heed, shifting his focus to the bags.

The kids had dropped them right where he'd told them to: near the entry to the alley and visible to anyone who passed, but likely to be written off quickly as garbage. They certainly weren't of interest enough that anyone should stop their car to inspect them, although a curious pedestrian might stop for a look. If that happened, he'd have to warn them off as quickly as he could.

Fortunately, the next twenty minutes passed uneventfully. A few cars passed, so did a handful of pedestrians, but nobody took any interest in the bags, if they even noticed them there at all. The whole time, Herron tapped a tune on the wheel, eager to see what he'd have to deal with when the pickup crew arrived.

"Showtime." Herron spotted a car in his rear-view. It slowed down as it passed him, then stopped right next to the bags by the alleyway. "Who do we have here?"

Unlike many of the cars in the area, this one was a far nicer model, a black Mercedes sedan that looked stupidly out of place in such a run-down part of town. It proved whoever oversaw the piracy operation lived a better life than Bautista and his ilk.

He stayed in his seat as the rear doors of the Mercedes opened and two suited Asian men climbed out. From this distance, he figured they were about twenty-five—too young to be the ringleaders but plenty old enough to be the muscle. They proved it a moment later when they hefted the bags into the trunk of the Mercedes, either not curious to check inside or ordered not to.

"Guess we're doing this the easy way..." Herron murmured. "For once."

If the goons had opened the bags and seen what was inside, it would've made following them much harder. As it was, he watched in silence as they loaded all six duffel bags inside the trunk and then slammed it closed. Less than sixty seconds after they'd climbed out of the car, the enforcers were getting back inside.

They hadn't even looked up and down the street to check the coast was clear.

Their lack of caution was a dead giveaway—these men thought they had nothing to fear. They thought the bags contained millions of dollars' worth of gold and platinum, and yet were totally confident they hadn't been scammed or that any cops might be waiting nearby to make an arrest. They operated with impunity, gods of their own domain, both betrayal and failure impossible.

Herron's bet that they were pros had paid off. They wouldn't know their duffel bags were full of trash until it was too late, nor that a predator was now on their tail. All their attempts at operational security using encrypted messages, burner cell phones, and hired hijackers unknown to each other had been blown totally to hell.

He hit the gas. The car responded with a cough, then slowly gained speed. As he inched closer to the Mercedes, he kept far enough back to not raise the alarm, but given the lack of traffic on the roads he didn't have to work very hard to stay on its tail.

Besides, even if he lost them, he had one more trick up his sleeve.

With one hand on the wheel, he dug through his

pocket and pulled out the phone he'd taken from the hijackers. His eyes flickered between the road and the phone screen as he opened an app that would let him track the Mercedes with the help of a five-buck key chain locator he'd purchased, paired to the phone, and then thrown into one bag.

So far, it looked like it would do the job just fine.

He followed the enforcers until they arrived at a low-density industrial area and pulled to a stop in front of a warehouse. Herron continued past it, even as the roller-door opened, and the Mercedes drove inside.

He parked further down the street. With one eye on his mirrors to make sure nobody emerged from the warehouse again, Herron counted to thirty and then climbed out of the car. He disappeared down an alleyway that ran down the side of the warehouse, moved around to the rear of the building, and searched for an entry point.

He found one quickly: a broken window that had been replaced with balsa. He needed to stand on a trash can to reach it, but once he did, it was child's play to remove the panel. He dropped it to the ground, then quickly and quietly climbed through the space.

When he had his feet on the ground inside, he put on his balaclava, drew his pistol, and got to work.

"OF ALL THE PLACES..."

Herron screwed up his nose. The further inside the warehouse he stalked, the more the smell of fish overwhelmed him. The stench made his eyes water, a final flourish to an interior that was already dark, dank, and dusty. It *also* made him want to rush, but to do so could lead to a mistake; instead, he sucked it up and kept going.

He'd entered via some sort of office, lit only by the light from the window behind him. The furniture was old and covered in dust, which suggested the warehouse hadn't been used for its original purpose for some time. It made sense the hijackers would base themselves somewhere unlikely to get attention, but a disused fish cannery?

What next? The mafia in a mausoleum? Terrorists in a tannery?

He pushed through the back areas of the warehouse quickly, confident everyone inside would be gathered around the car and eager to examine the bags the enforcers had collected. He still checked all the corners as he moved, keen to avoid an ambush, but he passed through several large rooms without incident.

He entered a larger space, a storeroom stripped of furniture, with boxes and bags full of assorted loot Herron could only assume had been pillaged from dozens of ships. There was cash, jewellery, bars of precious metals, plus some documents and a bunch of other stuff Herron hadn't thought pirates would be interested in, but which must have some sort of value.

It was a treasure trove of misery, plundered on the high seas.

He left the room with the loot and passed through more dank areas filled with rusted industrial machinery. The genuine mystery wasn't where he'd find the hijackers, but how he'd do it with his eyes watering so badly. How could a place that seemed so long out of operation still stink so badly? It was like the rotten-fish smell was baked into the concrete and the steel, destined to haunt the building no matter what purpose it served later.

The thought distracted him a little... enough that he almost got his head knocked off.

Some primal, reptilian instinct deep in the recesses of his brain warned him just in time, and he ducked as someone standing to the side of the doorway he'd passed through swung a steel pipe at him. The metal slammed into the wall—loud and harmless—but would have caused a mess had it connected.

"Strike!" Herron snarled. Returning to his full height, he shot his assailant in the gut with the silenced pistol, then cracked him over the head with the butt. "You're out."

With any pretence of stealth blown, Herron slid behind cover as a pair of heavies appeared and opened fire on him. He guessed that a second ago they had been gathered around the vehicle to open their bags of gold and was a little sad to have missed their moment of disappointment.

He kept low as shots slammed into the steel drum he was sheltered behind, the impromptu cover holding up so far.

"Police!" Herron shouted over the sound of the gunfire, hoping the heavies might be scared enough of the authorities to hesitate. All he got in return was more bullets. "Shit!"

"You're not the police." A female voice he knew well laughed derisively at his attempt to fake them out. "The man who tried to blow me up does not work for the police..."

The Widow.

"Oh hey, girlfriend!" Herron popped up, fired a few suppressed shots that hit one of the Widow's goons, then ducked back behind cover. "I'm here to finish the job."

"Looks like you're a little under manned for that." The rattle of a submachine gun and shots ricocheted off the drum. "But it saves my men from hunting you down..."

My men.

Was she more than just a rank-and-file pirate with delusions of self-importance?

Was she a leader?

Was she *the* leader?

The only way to find out was to capture her, the Widow, the clear next link in the path to the top.

That had been made harder because of the dumb luck of the guy who'd ambushed him. Now, instead of a sneak attack, he'd needed to overcome a numerically superior foe. He looked around for something to turn the tables on the hijackers.

Then he spotted it—a dozen fifty-five-gallon drums against the wall of the warehouse.

Near to the hijackers and their vehicle.

With the 'Flammable' symbol on them.

Taking his chance while he still had it, Herron pushed himself up and fired several shots over the top of his drum. They slammed into the chemical barrels, tearing holes that let the contents spew out over the floor. Crouching into cover again for a second, he repeated the process, until vast pools of the mystery fluid had spilled from the punctured drums. Then he pulled out his Zippo, lit it...

And threw it across the warehouse.

The chemicals ignited and in seconds the entire space was brightened by flames, before gradually blackening with smoke. This soup of misery made Herron's eyes water but was altogether worse for his foes, who were coughing and spluttering as they choked on the noxious clouds.

The distraction was enough to conceal him as he burst from behind the drum. A few shots whined towards him, but none of them found their mark. He returned fire, snapping off a shot at one heavy who'd abandoned his cover in the confusion. His aim was perfect, square between the eyes of his target. The man made no sound as he dropped, dead instantly.

Herron made it to the hood of the Mercedes and crouched down low. He scanned amidst the smoke and the flame for other threats, and a few shots pounded into the sedan. Down behind the engine block, he was safe for now, unless one of them managed to flank him.

"I'll give you one chance to put down your gun and come out into the open!" The voice of the Widow filled the cavernous warehouse. "Otherwise you're going to burn to death in here."

Herron laughed, sharp and bitter. "You clowns took away the only thing I cared about. There's nothing else you can do to hurt me. But there's plenty I can do that hurt you."

As he spoke, he spotted the last of the male goons, trying to sneak up on him from the side while the Widow distracted him with conversation. Herron shifted his aim and fired at the same time as his foe. The enforcer dropped, and Herron felt something hit him in the right shoulder. He grunted and reached up to the wound.

Just a graze.

Herron let out a sigh of relief. "Nobody else left to help you, lady."

"I assume you're the reason my team never reported in?" Somewhere in the thick smoke, she coughed. "That's a lot of valuable assets you've taken from me."

"You're the one who chews up men and spits them out!" Herron laughed. "I didn't realise you were the leader of this whole shindig, though."

"I sometimes like to get my hands dirty..."

"Well, now they're going to get bloody." Herron skirted around the car to the sound of her voice. "You shouldn't have assumed a yacht was easy prey. You never know who's aboard."

"And who might that be?"

Spotting her through the same smoke that concealed him from her, Herron took aim. He grinned, wrenched her weapon from her hand, then spun her round to face him. With the flames reflected in his eyes, he figured he must look like one scary motherfucker... but still she looked composed. Her eyes were cold, but there was something in them he hadn't seen on the yacht. Not fear. He doubted she ever showed that. Something more akin to curiosity or wonder.

Herron's lips curled into a thin smile. "You're a dead wom—"

Shouts filled the warehouse, and flashlights knifed through the smoke and darkness. Herron couldn't see much of the figures storming in, but there had to be a half-dozen or more of them.

Cops.

A SWAT team, he assumed.

And a damn fine one, given he hadn't heard a thing.

He kept his gun pressed against the Widow, but the new arrivals had changed the arithmetic of the situation. He hadn't planned to kill the woman right away; he wanted to see if she was indeed the end of the line, the top dog in the leadership structure of the hijackers. Now he might never get the chance to find out. And if he pulled the trigger, the police flooding the warehouse would blow him away.

With a sigh, Herron lowered his pistol and tossed it on the ground.

6

"**M**r Herron!"

"Why are you in the Philippines?"

"Do you regret your many crimes?"

"Is our president in danger?"

"Did the CIA send you?"

Herron squinted as camera flashes flared in his eyes and questions, shouted in broken English by a dozen journalists, assaulted his ears. He could do little beyond that to shield himself from the abuse, because his hands were cuffed behind him and a pair of burly cops had him in a tight grip, manhandling him past the assembled reporters.

After his arrest at the cannery, he'd been bundled into a cop car and driven into the capital—Manila—where he'd been paraded past a small media throng and into the police headquarters. The questions shouted at him had told him plenty: the authorities knew who he was and that he was wanted in a hundred countries.

It made his situation bleak and his efforts to extract himself from the spotlight more difficult.

As he was walked through the corridors of the colonial-era building, he couldn't help but feel some regret. He'd done his deal with Laidlaw to avoid exactly this kind of exposure.

They deposited him in a small, mostly featureless interview room. Besides a ceiling fan, which was protected from any shenanigans he might have in mind by a wire mesh cover, there was very little to work with, just a wooden table and four chairs, a mirror, a barred window, and the door. The only other thing was a camera in the corner of the room to monitor him.

"Boo." Herron jerked his head forward at one cop, startling both, then chuckled. "They clearly gave me the bench warmers..."

The cops didn't say a word, but he could tell they were furious. One pinned his arms while the other unlocked the handcuffs, quickly re-cuffed him to a steel ring on the table and then shoving him into the chair. Only then did the cops relax, step back and exhale. They had him as secure as could be, ready for whatever came next.

They shuffled out of the room and left Herron with only the camera to keep him company. Out of habit, he checked the cuffs, the metal ring, the feet of the table and the feet of the chair, but all were as secure as they needed to be.

Like it or not, he was stuck here for a while.

Herron settled in for the wait, because long experience had taught him his captors would show up when they damn well pleased. If he was in their position, he'd make his prisoner wait for hours. With that in mind, he closed his eyes and put his mind in neutral, content to recharge his batteries until he needed to pay attention again.

As he rested, he felt the temperature in the interview room rise steadily. The sun was beaming into the window and the small fan did little to help. An hour passed, then hours, until finally he grew impatient. He'd had no food or water. He'd had no bathroom breaks. The combined message of all of this was clear—he was being softened up.

It was nearly another hour before the thick door unlocked with a clunk and squealed open on its hinges. Two cops walked inside, both male, their faces neutral as they sat opposite him. They got settled, chatting to each other in their own language, then fixed him with a hard gaze.

"What is your business in our country, Mr Herron?" One man, probably the senior detective, leaned forward and rested his elbows on the table. "You're not welcome here."

Herron kept quiet.

"You were arrested trespassing on private property, where we also found several bodies and a fire you lit..." The detective let out a fake-weary sigh. "Even without your other crimes abroad, you're in a lot of trouble."

He'd already tuned out. He'd been tortured by the best of them—an Iranian known only as Pain, an artist of her craft. Civilian law enforcement couldn't compare, even in places where the law might sometimes inch over the line a little. They'd have to go a lot further than that to get him to say a word.

Realising his prisoner wasn't listening, the detective pounded his fist on the table. "You need to work with us, Mr Herron!"

Herron didn't flinch at the action; he just closed his eyes, took a deep breath—slowly in and slowly out—and then opened them again and stared at the detective. "I don't *need* to do anything."

The detective's face screwed up in frustration. "Suit yourself, but we're the one thing standing between you and extradition to one of many countries where the punishment for your crimes will be death..."

Herron snorted. He'd cheated death so many times, the thought of it didn't scare him at all. He'd rather avoid it for now, but it didn't frighten him as it might other people. "Let's spin the wheel to see where I go."

"No need." The other cop laughed, his paunch jiggling in time with his joviality. "That's already been decided."

"And they're *burning* to meet you..." The lead detective joined in on the joke at Herron's expense. "You really should have gone to the bottom of the ocean with your yacht."

Herron's mind worked overtime to decipher what they'd said. The clues were obvious, because they clearly couldn't help themselves, so it was more a sense-check on if they were telling the truth. Laidlaw had told him that the Philippine Government hadn't lifted a finger to stop the hijackers, but the detectives' less than subtle references told him more than that.

It told him they were in league with the Widow and her pirates.

Suddenly, it made some sense. The cops had *saved* the Widow, not *arrested* her. He seriously doubted now that she was in the next room being subjected to the same treatment as he was.

Sure, no criminal organisation could act with such impunity without having someone in the authorities in its pocket, but the comments from both detectives told him this relationship was more than that. It was more permissive and more coordinated.

Herron smiled at the detectives. "A steak, fries and a coffee."

They looked at each other in confusion. At last, the one with the paunch spoke. "What?"

"If you get me a steak, some fries and a cup of coffee, I'll tell you anything you want to know."

Their eyes lit up, and it was easy to understand why. They had the collar of their career in the seat opposite them: the most wanted man on the planet, a man they clearly expected to be extradited as any moment. Yet he'd just offered to spill the beans in return for a trivial boon... and that gave them the chance to be famous.

The older detective nodded, and they stood and left the room.

This time, it didn't take long for them to return. A half-hour later, the door screeched open again, and the cops entered; this time, one of them carried a tray with a plate on it, filled with a large steak and all the fries Herron could ever hope to eat. The other carried a takeaway coffee cup from Starbucks–a franchise that had obviously made it to Manila.

They'd gone to a lot of effort to please him, on the promise he'd deliver more in return.

Herron watched as the plate, the coffee and some flatware were put in front of him. He waited for them to return to their seats, then made a show of trying to eat with his hands cuffed to the table. With a sigh, he put the cutlery down and sat back in his chair, to make it clear he wouldn't talk until he could eat.

Again, the two detectives looked at each other. Herron could understand their hesitation but was counting on their greed for fame to overcome it. On the one hand, he was well known as a deadly operator; Interpol's Red Notice said as much. But, even without cuffs, he was in a secure room, in the middle of a large police station, with a camera and two armed detectives watching him.

They'd be wondering: what's the worst he could do?

Eventually, they relented. One stood and backed away from the table, his hand on his sidearm. The other stood and moved around the table to Herron's side, reached into his pocket and pulled out the keys to the handcuffs. A second later, free of the restraints, Herron could enjoy the steak and the coffee.

He took his time with the meal because he didn't know when he'd get his next one. He savoured each morsel and washed it down with the hot coffee. It was so slow and rhythmic, the cops gradually let their guard down, content that they'd held up their end of the bargain and that Herron would soon hold up his.

When the steak was down to the last pieces, Herron lifted the fork to his mouth with one hand and gripped the serrated knife with the other. He smiled up at the guards. "I'm done."

* * *

"TIME TO TALK..." The detective against the wall grumbled. He started forward, grabbed Herron's plate, and held his hand out for the flatware. "Give me the knife."

He kept totally still as the other guard closed in with his colleague, cuffs out and ready to secure him to the table again. If that happened—if Herron was again disarmed and restrained—he wasn't sure he'd get another chance to get out of the situation. That meant he'd have to take down two cops who'd simply done their job, no matter how corrupt they might be. He'd have seconds to act—any slower, and whoever might be watching on the other side of the mirror or via the camera would summon help.

He waited until the detectives got close... then burst into life.

He had a simple plan, and he executed it with a speed that was a blur to the cops.

First, Herron rammed the serrated knife through the outstretched hand of the first cop, boring through the palm and into the wooden table. It pinned him in place as he screamed and grasped for the blade, too focused on his pain to draw his weapon.

Second, he kicked out at the knee of the man trying to cuff him. The detective let out a pained scream, dropped the cuffs and collapsed to the ground like an avalanche down a mountainside, equally unable to grab his weapon.

Third, Herron lunged at the standing cop, who by now was trying to pull the knife from his hand. He snagged the pistol from the detective's holster and cracked it over the man's head, catching him just as he removed the knife.

With one down, Herron then moved to take the weapon of the cop he'd kneecapped.

Except, this time, things didn't go to plan.

His eyes widened as the cop's hand gripped the pistol a split-second before he could reach it. As the crippled detective drew the gun and prepared to aim, Herron only had a moment to act... and he did, with extreme violence.

His boot came down on the man's wrist, breaking it. The detective howled and released his grip on the pistol. Herron kicked the weapon away. "Stay down."

His former captor relented, clearly not wanting to add a third injury to his litany of misery. He glared at Herron. "You're not getting out of here alive."

"I'll take my chances." Herron crouched down to pick up the second pistol, then turned his back on both cops and aimed at the mirror. "You've got three seconds to duck."

He counted down silently in his head, then fired a single shot into the top of the glass. The pane shattered and fell in large pieces to the floor, where it blew into a thousand pieces.

Herron barely noticed. He grinned wolfishly as he looked through at the room on the other side of the broken mirror—or, more precisely, at the *person* on the other side of it.

"You're mine!" Herron snarled at the Widow, who was still half-ducked to avoid being shot. "No matter how many corrupt cops you put in my way."

She turned and ran from the room.

Herron swore and vaulted through the space vacated by the broken mirror. The shards of glass scratched and cut him in a few places on the way through, but the pain didn't register.

Who *was* this woman? And how did she have such influence over the local police?

Beyond the room, the police station was almost empty. It was well after midnight, so there were only a few cops on duty, and all of them were frozen in place, confused and surprised by the gunshots. It was the only thing that saved him from being pounced on by a few dozen officers.

The Widow was right ahead of him, and every bit as quick on her feet as he was. They passed offices and open-plan cubicles before bursting out the front door and onto the street. By the time he pushed outside after her, the Widow had flagged down a car and used her own pistol to force the driver out.

Herron pulled up short and looked around as she sped off. "Shit."

His own choices were limited, with no civilian cars in sight. His only option was a parked cop car, which wouldn't be the most inconspicuous getaway vehicle, but the cops inside the station would be right behind him...

He broke the car window, popped the door, and swiftly hot-wired the ride. The engine roared, and he slipped behind the wheel, jamming his foot to the floor.

Behind him, the police had finally spilled into the street and half a dozen shots cracked after him. None hit anything important, and soon enough Herron was far enough away that the gunfire didn't make a difference.

Of all the things he'd thought he might be doing the week after he left Fiji, a car chase in a stolen cop car wasn't one of them.

He could see the Widow's stolen car off in the distance. She tore through intersections without care for traffic, putting herself and others at significant risk. Herron had no choice but to follow, red lights be damned. He held his breath each time he approached an intersection and loudly exhaled each time he made it to the other side. The squad car was faster than the stolen sedan, and slowly but surely, he was making up ground...

... at least until another police squad car at one of those same intersections spotted the pursuit.

* * *

"SHIT." Herron winced as the cop car that was hot on his tail sped up hard enough to nudge his rear bumper. "Can't you just leave it?"

The chase that had taken them through the streets of Manila had now turned into a giant game of chicken, with Herron forced to weave between traffic, dodge parked cars and run lights to keep up. The Widow was a madwoman with a total disregard for her own safety, forcing him to push his vehicle to the absolute limits.

The nudge failed to force him off the road, his car veering off course slightly, but straightened by a quick adjustment of the wheel. He wasn't sure his luck would continue, but for now the cop backed off and took up station ten yards back. The officer had delivered his message to Herron that they could take him out at any time they wanted. It was better to give it up.

Herron had other ideas. He hadn't gotten this close to the Widow—twice now—only to let her bail again. He was hot on her tail; she wasn't much of a driver, so it wasn't difficult to keep up, but even as he got closer to her—and to the answers he sought—he couldn't just focus on the threat ahead.

Not with so many problems behind him as well.

One pursuer had turned into two and then into many, as squad cars scrambled from stations across the capital and moved to intercept him. Thankfully, they weren't coordinated enough to put roadblocks or spike strips in his way—yet—but the longer this went on, the more chance there was they'd get organized. Then he'd have a real problem.

If the cops weren't mad enough that he'd taken down a pair of detectives and bolted from their station, the theft of a car and a chase across Manila were sure to top off their outrage gauge. They'd been made to look like fools hours after he'd been paraded in front of the local media and the authorities had made it clear he'd be extradited. Only a quick capture would salve their egos.

And hide the fact that they were in league with the Widow and her hijackers.

As he shifted gear, gained speed and darted in between civilian vehicles, Herron tried to think through *that* link fully. He couldn't explain the Widow's presence on the other side of the two-way mirror, not exactly. How did she get an all-access pass to the police station and the interview? Did the hijacker chain of command go a lot higher than he'd first thought?

Laidlaw *had* said that the President had refused to act against them...

He continued to push the cop car to the upper limits of its speed, his eyes locked onto the Widow's car ahead. The strobing lights of the squad cars in his rear-vision mirror were a distraction, as was the wail of a half-dozen sirens, which were doing more to wake up every citizen in the capital than bring his car to a halt.

Up ahead, the road branched at a Y-shaped intersection. Herron's eyes narrowed—the police had finally got their act together, with roadblocks set up across both roads. Two squad cars were parked across each lane, while spike strips were deployed in front of them. Of most concern were the dozen cops with their weapons drawn, prepared to fill Herron and his ride with holes.

It gave him, and the Widow, mere seconds to choose a path.

Her choice would reveal a lot.

The seconds ticked down and, as he'd expected, she didn't amend her course, seemingly content to hit the roadblock and trust her friends in the police force would take care of her, the situation and the threat Herron posed. He figured about twenty seconds before she hit the roadblock, so he had little time to choose.

In the end, it only took him two.

The cop cars in pursuit peeled off as he approached the roadblock. That was standard, but they did it too early, and that told Herron they'd been ordered to keep plenty of distance. And the only reason for that would be because they knew his car would soon be filled with lead. They wanted to avoid collateral damage.

They'd pursued him closely and fired a few shots to keep him honest, but their main game was the roadblock up ahead, a trap they were corralling him into. And he'd driven right into it. He cursed himself for having such tunnel vision for the chase but knew now at least he had to take urgent action, to get himself clear of danger and the Widow out of the safe embrace of the law.

Their trap sprung, the cops obviously didn't think he could do it, but Herron had made a career out of impossible actions. He shifted his focus to the Widow's car up ahead. Only a dozen yards in front, it was speeding for the roadblock.

Herron floored the accelerator. The engine roared in response and the police cruiser jerked forward. He closed in on the sedan and got his hood next to the rear left corner of the vehicle.

"Time to see if you can pass your stunt licence."

He jerked the wheel suddenly and smashed violently into the Widow's car.

The damaged vehicle skidded under the impact, then veered left as she overcompensated. Herron kept his eyes on her vehicle as he steered away, then back into her, then again. On the third impact, she spun the car out and barely avoided crashing into a parked vehicle as she screeched to a halt.

But in his desperation to get her, Herron had screwed up as well.

He looked ahead and saw a car stopped at a set of lights. He was approaching too fast to avoid a collision, so he stiffened and braced for the impact he knew was coming. His cop car collided with the stationary vehicle with a sickening crunch and his head slammed into the airbag.

Coughing as the bag deflated, Herron cursed. "Damn it!"

He extracted himself from behind the wheel, the seatbelt and the mashed car as quickly as he could, stopping only briefly to see that the driver of the vehicle in front of him was okay. Satisfied, he turned and raised his pistol at the Widow's vehicle, which he'd left a few dozen yards back.

Her car was a mess, but she'd already got out of it. He saw her running away from him, down the street and into an alleyway, clearly knowing she'd caught a break and not wasting time looking back at him.

Herron cursed and ran after her.

7

T he smart thing to do would be to bug out.

He could lie low for a few weeks, steal a boat and get far away from the Philippines, where the cops knew his name, the media had broadcast his location, and it was likely every enemy he'd ever had would soon be on a plane to look for him.

But Herron couldn't give up. His pledge to Laidlaw made this a mission... and he'd never once failed to complete a mission. Sure, he'd partially disrupted the hijackers' operation, killed almost a dozen of them on board his own yacht and another bunch on the container ship, but if the Widow got away, the job would only be partially completed.

The spider would still have its head.

She'd hatch more eggs.

Put others in danger.

And so he gave chase.

His arms pistoned and his legs chewed up the distance in great strides as he powered after her. She surprised him with how nimble she was, but he was making up the ground quickly, until she looked over her shoulder, smiled and broke left into a crowded marketplace.

Herron groaned as he followed her. "Give me a break…"

Not quite the tin-roof shanty market common throughout Asia, it was hardly a luxury shopping destination either. Each stall was a dozen feet wide and almost as deep, selling everything from tourist trinkets to clothing to fresh produce, meat, and fish—the entire spectrum of life.

Herron's sole focus, however, was on the Widow.

He pushed past one shopper and then another who'd ambled into his path. He shouted at them to get out of the way. Most heeded his call, but one didn't—an elderly man wandered in front of him, pushing a shopping cart. Herron barrelled into it, toppling it over.

As vegetables and groceries littered the ground, the old man also collapsed under the impact. Feet slipping on squashed tomatoes and bananas, the old man clutching at his jacket for help, Herron slowed only long enough to ease the man to the ground, then sprinted off after the Widow as onlookers stared.

But that second or two spent helping the old guy had proven costly, because he'd lost sight of her. She'd be well ahead of him now, perhaps impossible to catch. If bailing on the mission was the smart thing for him to do, the same was surely true for her, and if she disappeared now, he'd struggle to find her again.

He pushed deeper into the market, jostling more shoppers, eyes sweeping the crowds. He looked inside market stalls, amongst the people, and in every corner and shadow. But the market was cavernous—potentially the largest in Manila—and the Widow was nowhere to be seen.

The one fact in his favour was that the market was a labyrinth. His sense of direction was excellent, but even he had been turned around more than once by the uncoordinated distribution of the stalls and the walkway. It was the sort of disorganised, unplanned and organic layout locals would navigate in their sleep, but anyone foreign to the market—Herron and, he hoped, the Widow—could be tripped up by.

It gave him a chance, albeit not a very good one.

He pulled up short at a map of the market stuck to a concrete wall. It was covered in text he couldn't understand, but the diagrammatic outline of the market was easy enough to interpret in any language. It showed the maze of stalls and four exits, one at each point of the compass.

Four chances to catch her. One correct choice. He had to gamble.

With each moment of hesitation, each second studying the map, the Widow moved further away, but he had to choose correctly. He disregarded the southern exit, through which they'd entered; it was less likely she'd double back. He also ruled out the eastern exit because it led out to a large park. The open spaces would probably have fewer people than the tight concentration of bodies on Manila's bustling streets.

No, if she chose well, she'd pick the exit that took her to the streets, somewhere she could hide in the crowd long enough to melt away forever.

Herron took a moment more to decide between the northern and western exits, settling on the latter. He figured there was a greater chance the Widow would try to change direction rather than heading directly south to north. It wasn't a confident bet, but he had to make a call quickly and get on with the chase.

He set off through the market, painfully aware of the time he'd just lost considering his options. He ran down the stallholder walkway to steal some time back, a route reserved for staff and owners of stalls. Shouts and curses followed him as he passed pitch after pitch, weaving between boxes of everything from fruit to home wares.

As he neared the western exit, he spotted her. She was fighting her way through the crowd with far less success than he had, and for once, Herron was glad to be the obnoxious American, visible to all and loathed for his brashness. Sacrificing politeness meant he'd made better time.

Herron followed her outside, far enough back and in amongst the crowd that she didn't notice him when she checked behind her, despite the locals tutting and glaring as he barrelled past them. He inched closer to her; she was good, but he was better, content to bide his time even as cop cars blazed past and headed towards his last-known location.

It didn't matter; they'd already lost containment, and he had their prize in his sights.

When the last of the cop cars had passed, he picked up his pace and moved within striking distance of the Widow. With each passing second, he expected her to look over her shoulder, spot him, and run. He'd give chase if that happened... but it didn't. Now she was clear of the market, she was once more confident in herself and her position.

She was a criminal leader, supported by the cops and the government.

She did not need to run.

Or so she thought.

Close enough at last, and not caring who saw him do it, Herron grabbed her around the neck and jammed his pistol into her back. "Toss your gun into the trash can."

The Widow struggled as much as Herron's headlock permitted, croaking an appeal for help. But while several of the locals had spotted what was happening, they gave the pair a wide berth, scuttling away nervously. Herron noticed a few had pulled out their cell phones to film him or call the cops, but he ignored them. He planned to be long gone before the cops doubled back to his location.

"The gun." Herron squeezed her throat tighter and pressed the gun into her harder. "I will not ask again."

She finally complied. Moving slowly so Herron wouldn't be spooked and put a bullet in her, she reached into her purse and removed the pistol she'd used to hijack the car. Lifting it from the tip of the barrel using her thumb and index finger, she was careful not to get anywhere near the trigger. A second later, the gun was in a trash can and Herron had a grin on his face.

But it disappeared as he looked around for transport options, because he noticed where they were.

Just across the road from them stood the Chinese Embassy.

His eyes shifted to the Embassy gate and the CCTV cameras positioned above it, and suddenly Herron knew everything he needed to know. The Widow's plea for help hadn't been aimed at the passers-by around them, but the Embassy security team that would be alert for anything outside their walls.

"I wondered why the head of a piracy racket was being treated like a VIP by the cops..." Herron muttered. "But now it's all so much clearer to me."

When she kept quiet in response to his suggestive accusation, Herron kept that discussion on ice. There'd be all the time in the world for it later; for now, he was keen to get away before the police responded to the calls from those concerned citizens. But in the moment he was distracted, she finally made her move.

Herron cried out in pain as a small blade dug into his thigh: a concealed knife the Widow had produced from somewhere. He'd lazily assumed she was unarmed, because if she'd had a gun she would have used it before now, but he'd been so overcome by a red haze of anger that he'd neglected to frisk her.

It was a rookie mistake that might prove deadly.

*   *   *

As he winced, distracted by the pain, an elbow slammed into his stomach, and his grip loosened just enough for the Widow to slip free.

"Bitch," he spat. "You're dead."

She backed away from him, the small knife in her hand poised to strike, a broad smile on her flushed-red face. "You had your chance. You took too long. Now you're mine."

Herron raised his pistol to finish her once and for all, but again, he hesitated. He needed her alive for a little longer yet, to make sure he'd taken the head off the piracy ring. She had other ideas. A second of delay was all she needed to be in his face, slashing out at the hand that held the pistol, the razor-sharp blade cutting once, twice.

Herron cursed as his fingers released the pistol. It hit the ground and she kicked it away, but he could do nothing to retrieve it because she was on him. The blade danced in her hands, probing his defences and slicing, all the while onlookers gasping and crying out in panic around them. He could do little more than fend away the more serious strikes, each time taking a cut for his troubles, the old truism proving true.

In a knife fight, one person ends up cut, and the other ends up dead.

Backing away to give himself the space and time to keep her at bay, he stole a split-second glance around them. The gates of the Embassy were still closed, so nobody was coming to help her, but nobody on the street was looking to aid him either. The cops were getting closer, judging by the sirens, and there was nothing immediate to hand for him to use as a weapon of his own.

He took another cut.

Another.

Another.

His blood was flowing freely now, the deep wound in his thigh combining with a half-dozen shallow ones to stain his clothing and leave small dribbles on the sidewalk as he retreated from her. He hadn't taken any critical wounds—yet—but each slowed him down and gave her a little more ascendency.

Confident and in control, she grinned as another swift stab went close to skewering him. "If you turn and run, I won't follow."

"Fuck you." Herron kicked out, landing only a glancing blow, but forcing her back a step. "This ends now."

Herron was tired of running...

... and hiding...

... and denying his nature.

Determined to make a stand, despite his injuries and the lack of conditioning from long months spent on his yacht, he felt a fire in his stomach that fuelled his movements. He darted back from another slash, blindly reaching out to grab a raincoat from a rack out front of a street stall, a two-buck covering against Manila's frequent tropical storms that Herron hoped would protect him better than that.

He quickly rolled the jacket into a ball and then changed up the game.

He came at her, using the balled-up jacket like a shield as the Widow slashed out at him again. The blade buried itself in the jacket, robbed of its power, but Herron still felt another sting in his hand as the tip of the blade bit into him. This wound was nothing compared to what he'd gained in return—control. The Widow's eyes widened in fear as she realized the power shift, and he struck.

He reached out with his free hand to grab her wrist and snapped it. She cried out in pain and released her grip on the knife, which remained buried in the coat.

Herron yanked on it at the cost of a deeper cut, but finally disarmed her. Now the tables had turned. He didn't let up, closing the distance between them and delivering a brutal knee to her midsection. She yelped and doubled over, then put her back in a headlock.

Except, this time, she was out of tricks.

"We're going for a walk." Herron gripped her tight and looked around. No cops. No embassy goons. No bystanders looking to intervene. "Try to escape again and I'll snap your neck."

She didn't respond. She was done fighting back —for now.

He dragged her into the street, in front of the slow amble of cars that clogged the narrow roads around the market. Vehicles approached in both directions, but Herron saw the one he wanted in the southbound lane —a newer model Mercedes. He marched the Widow toward the car, bleeding and angry, ready to take issue with the driver if he had to.

Herron stood in the way, and the driver slowed the car to a stop. The man took a second to take in the scene in front of him, then held his hands in plain sight, just above the wheel. Herron gestured with his chin: get the hell out of the car or get hurt. The driver did so without hesitation, running from the situation as fast as his legs could carry him.

Herron opened the rear door, punched the Widow hard enough to knock her out, then shoved her inside. "Time to go."

* * *

It was night by the time he parked the Mercedes. He'd driven them from the market at top speed, darting between traffic and working his ass off to the evade the cops, the Widow unconscious on the back seat. It had taken some time, but the high-performance vehicle had served him well and within an hour he'd been free of police attention.

He'd pulled over and opened the trunk, hoping to find something to tie up his captive. Inside, there was a bunch of junk; the owner of the car was clearly some sort of hoarder or survivalist. There was a tow-rope—which he'd used immediately to bind the Widow—a tool kit, a reserve gas can, a tire iron, some emergency flares, a blanket, a first aid kit and more. He'd been forced to shift it all to the back seat to make enough room to lock the woman in the trunk.

And now he opened it again, looked down at her and smiled. "Good evening. Have a nice sleep?"

"Mmm!" She tried to speak, but Herron had stuffed another of his discoveries—an oily rag—in her mouth. She didn't bother to test the rope tying her hands and ankles together, her broken wrist making such efforts futile. "Mmm!"

He lifted her out and tossed her roughly onto the forest floor. Then he knelt down next to her. "What happens next is up to you, so I suggest you answer my questions."

She continued to stare up at him with cold, fearless eyes. Herron respected that—even though he'd bested her and her network of hijackers, she at least had some self-respect.

It wouldn't matter a few hours from now, when he'd done what he had to do to get the answers he needed, but for now, he had to give her a little credit.

The moment he removed the gag from her mouth, however, the source of her impressive confidence was revealed. She smiled. "I'm a Chinese diplomat. Holding me prisoner violates the law."

"So does coordinating the hijacking of a few dozen

vessels in international waters." Herron sneered. "You're a smart woman. You've done your homework."

"Of course."

"Then you know what I did to China Offshore Oil and Gas in Fiji." Herron leaned in close to her face. "You think I give a damn about your diplomatic immunity?"

Less than a month ago, he'd blown up a gas facility owned by the state-owned China Offshore Oil and Gas Company. He'd cost the company billions, removed its stranglehold over Fijian politics, and brought a swift end to the reign of the local dictator.

She stiffened, and for the second time in a few hours, Herron detected fear in her. Who knew what such a man would be capable of here, deep in the forest, with no witnesses?

"I can't say anything to you." All the earlier bravado had vanished from her voice. "It's treason."

"Traitor if you talk, dead if you don't."

He needed information from this woman to deliver on his commitment to Laidlaw and, if she didn't provide it, he'd have to take her out. He couldn't think of anyone who deserved it more: a middle manager protected by diplomatic immunity. She preyed on the vulnerable by choice, made *others* prey on the vulnerable to put food on their table. That made her expendable.

"I want to know why a Chinese diplomat is coordinating hijackings." He walked to the car and grabbed the tire iron he'd shifted from the trunk to the back seat. "I'm prepared to work for the answer."

"Because the Foreign Ministry told me to," she snapped. "Because, like everything else that's happening in the waters of Southeast Asia, China wants its neighbours to cry for help or run in fear."

Herron's eyes widened. "So you want the United States Navy to struggle to stop the hijackers. The President of the Philippines will beg China for help and the problem will magically disappear."

"Sure..." Her voice trailed off, like she was thinking better of what she was about to say. "A few low-level deaths and a few destroyed hijacker vessels will have them eating out of the Party's hand."

It had been the same story in Fiji: China had propped up the General—a brutal military dictator—in return for the right to exploit his country's resources. Clearly, the country was flexing its muscles across Asia, using a range of plots and mechanisms to exert control. It was behaviour consistent with an emerging great power and eventually it would lead to a clash with the US.

And the more the US pushed to counter it, the more the Philippines, Fiji, and places like them would fall into China's lap.

"I'm going to need more than that if you want to make it out of here with your head on your shoulders." Herron slapped the tire iron against his palm. "I need answers."

"No need to be so crude." She spoke carefully, her eyes on the weapon in his hand. "My entire career has been about making deals. So let's make one."

"I'm listening. But you better give me something damn interesting, otherwise bits of you are going to break until you do."

"What do you want?"

"Your bosses. You can save your own skin by giving up whoever's in charge of the smuggling operation."

"You may as well just kill me, then. I'd prefer that to the punishment for betraying the Party."

She didn't know how tempted he was to do just that. His whole being wanted him to swing the tire iron at her skull, take vengeance for the things and the people she'd taken from him—the things and the people she'd taken from *others*—and stop her from doing ever again.

She undoubtedly deserved it.

She was proud of her work and certain of her cause.

She had no remorse for anything she'd done.

She'd continue to do it.

He lifted the tire iron to strike.

And the Widow's head exploded.

8

Herron flinched as blood and brain matter sprayed his face.

He blinked in confusion, looked down at the tire iron, then back at the Widow's corpse. What used to be her head was now a mess of gore, flayed skin, and matted hair—far more damage than could be inflicted by a crude weapon like a tire iron.

Especially given he hadn't hit her with it.

In a split-second, his mind finally caught up to his eyes. He ducked low to obstruct the sniper's next shot, winced as the shot bored deep into the trunk of a nearby tree and told him the direction of the shooter.

South.

Grasping the tire iron—his only weapon against the sniper—Herron ran back to the car and took shelter behind the hood. Inhaling sharply, he pressed his back against the vehicle, even as the sniper fired a half-dozen rounds into the engine and destroyed his ability to escape.

He assessed his situation. It was clear now why the

Widow hadn't put up more of a fight once he'd taken her out of the trunk. She'd thought an embassy wet team would follow them and bail her out.

Instead, they'd been deployed to blow her head off.

In the end, her self-proclaimed ability to control the men around her had let her down.

That was cold comfort for Herron. His situation was bleak: he was alone in a country he didn't know well, with just a tire iron and his wits to defend himself against an entrenched sniper with a suppressed, high-calibre weapon. Nothing else could cause the amount of damage to the Widow's skull without a sound.

The only consolation was that the shooter had taken out the Widow first. If Herron had been the first target, he'd be with his maker right now.

That fact alone suggested he was dealing with an embassy wet asset. The Filipino police would have taken him down straight away, especially given he was holding a heavy tool up, ready to kill their honoured guest. The Embassy would consider the Widow to be a burned asset. They'd worry she'd talk to Herron, so she'd have to die first. It wasn't a certainty, but that's where he'd have his money.

Now he was alone in the woods with no means of escape from one or more enemy operatives.

Armed enemy operatives.

Deniable enemy operatives.

It wasn't the worst situation he'd ever been in, but it was near the top of the list. Almost all the other times, he'd had more weaponry or more support, but there was neither on offer here. That reduced his chances of success against his hidden foe to near zero.

He waited for more shots to land, but except for the

gentle rustle of trees in the breeze, the forest was silent. The shooter was seemingly content to wait for Herron to get impatient and put himself in the crosshairs, or else keep a close eye on him until the rest of the operators arrived to kill him.

With a sigh, Herron decided he needed to make a move.

He had to play a hunch, one he knew would get him killed if he'd guessed wrong. Taking the chance, he peered up above the engine block. His head was exposed for a good five seconds, more than enough time for a shooter to spot him and take him out.

No shot came.

He let out a long exhale. "Thermal imaging."

The shooter had a thermal scope, but he couldn't see when Herron popped up over the engine, which had until a few minutes ago been working its ass off and burning hot. But he knew that moving away from the engine would instantly reveal him to the shooter.

Unless...

The seed of an idea forming in his head, Herron moved carefully to the back seat of the car, knowing his heat signature would no longer be hidden and that a shot from a high-calibre rifle could punch through any part of the car that wasn't the engine.

He opened the door and winced as a shot ricocheted off the vehicle, but he didn't delay in grabbing the few items he needed—the half-full reserve gas can and the box of flares.

Working quickly along the side of the car, more shots pounding into the vehicle, he opened the cap for the gas tank. Knowing he was taking a huge chance, he lit one flare, shoved it into the tank, and ran like crazy.

As shots bored into the car and trees around him, Herron bolted through the forest, knowing he needed to get far away from the vehicle. A second later, the car exploded in a massive fireball as its gas tank ignited.

And, for a split second, the entire forest was lit up by a blinding flash.

Knowing the sort of discomfort the blast would have caused anyone watching through a thermal scope—searing and painful—Herron had a few seconds of total freedom. He moved further to the south, darting between trees, making use of every moment he was free from the sniper's fire.

"Good shooter..." Herron whispered to himself as he pressed up against the trunk of a tree and tossed the empty gas can on the ground. "But not great..."

The whole time he'd been running, he'd been spilling gas from the reserve tank over the forest floor. And now, hoping he had got none of the fuel on his clothing, he prepared for his last play.

He sparked the last of his two flares and tossed it on the liquid.

The result was muted at first. The flare ignited the gasoline, but it took some time for the forest to burn properly. Thirty seconds. A minute. Two. But eventually the flames, aided by the fuel, began to consume the forest, the blaze growing with each passing second.

And each passing second making thermal imagining less effective.

Herron waited as long as he dared, knowing a kill team of operatives might be on their way, then took his chance. Although he wanted to kill the sniper, his mission to destroy the piracy ring was completed, and it was time to bug out. He wouldn't waste the chance he'd created for himself by being stupid.

He moved to the north, back in the car's direction, the flames in between himself and the sniper. The thermal shroud he'd covered himself in did the trick: the shooter couldn't find a target amongst the flames and he clearly had no other type of scope amongst his gear.

He was blind... and Herron was out of there.

* * *

NOW A MILE PAST THE CAR, Herron continued through the forest, his footfalls as silent as whispers, each move careful. He was free of the shackles of the sniper's gaze, but now he had other problems. He had no vehicle, it was a long way back to the road, and he knew a kill team might be hunting him.

His bag of tricks empty, he was fumbling through the forest in near-total darkness. He could see only a few feet ahead of him, using the small amount of light from the moon that peeked through the canopy, and knew any operatives tracking him would have thermal imaging he could no longer spoof.

As he moved, his senses worked their hardest to locate the hunters he assumed were out there—his ears for any sound, his eyes for any movement, his nose for any scent. If he detected someone, he could get the jump on them or evade them entirely, but it was just as likely they'd kill him before he even knew they were there.

Fifteen minutes later, resting against a tree, he heard the first potential contact: the muffled sound of a male voice. It carried farther than it usually would in the silence and stillness of the forest, the first sign the team arrayed against him was less than elite.

The operative should have known better. Herron would be sure to teach him.

He stayed pressed against the trunk of a tree, on the far side of where he thought the voice came from. If he was wrong, the operative would likely have seen him already with the thermal goggles. When no shots came, he figured he was as concealed as he could hope to be.

Crouching down, he fumbled on the ground until he found a small branch. He tapped the stick against the tree a few times and, after a half-dozen knocks, tossed it right in front of him. More noise for the operative to pick up on.

More chatter.

Male voice.

Close.

Herron remained deathly still. The operative came closer, the voice replaced by the sound of footfalls. He was good — quiet and slow — but he wasn't perfect, making a slight sound with every step. Each rustle of leaves was an imperfection Herron could make fatal.

When he was almost level with the tree, Herron swung the tire iron with all his strength.

The blow landed like an atom bomb. Although Herron's aim was a little low, for a blind attack he'd done enough. The steel crushed the man's oesophagus and he started to choke, even as he stumbled back in shock. Experience or instinct kicked in and the wounded man raised his submachine gun.

Herron gave him no time to aim and shoot. He gripped the tire iron tight, then brought it down on the operative's right hand, shattering his wrist and devastating the many other tiny bones nearby. The shock wave ensured he couldn't grip the submachine gun or pull the trigger.

As the operative screamed out in distress, Herron hit him one more time, a hard shot to the chin that knocked him out and sent him to the ground. Herron dropped on him, placing the bar lengthwise across his neck, and pressing down hard.

The unconscious man couldn't fight or struggle. It was over quickly.

The job done, Herron tossed the tire iron away and searched the corpse, fast but thorough. The thermal goggles and earpiece communicators the operatives were using were both perfectly intact. He put both on, then hefted the suppressed submachine gun.

And with the playing field levelled, he set off into the forest.

Figuring the dead operative's cry would bring the others down on top of him, Herron kept his eyes peeled. He could hear them talking and guessed it was Mandarin, pegging the team as Chinese.

Through the goggles, the trees and the ground looked dark, cool in the frigid night. Then a flash of colour.

A human.

The bright shape raised its weapon at the same time as he did, but a fraction of a second slower. The submachine gun kicked into Herron's shoulder, the suppressor stealing most of the discharge. Bullets ripped into the operative, and he dropped a moment before he could get his own shot off.

Herron looked around to make sure he was still

alone, then he closed in on the downed man. Although his victim was still, Herron put another couple of rounds into his head to be sure, removing the risk of a hidden knife—he wouldn't make that mistake again in a hurry—or a loud scuffle. Then he stripped the corpse of two extra magazines and departed.

As he searched the forest, he did a mental stock take. In his experience, special operations teams the world over mostly worked in groups of four. It allowed for a mix of specialisations and mission redundancy in the event of casualties, while keeping the size of teams and their missions manageable.

If he was right, he'd evaded the sniper and taken down two of the squad...

One to go.

* * *

FIFTEEN MINUTES LATER, frustration was gnawing at him. He'd located and downed two operatives without the tools to do so; now he had the right gear, but he'd failed to find the last man standing between him and freedom.

He let out a sigh. "Where are you?"

As he continued through the forest, he thought through a range of scenarios. The chatter in Mandarin over the comms had stopped, which meant they knew he was on the prowl or he was correct about their numbers, and the last man knew he had no one left to talk to. He scanned left and right, but the night vision goggles showed all dull and dark colours.

There was no telltale brightness to signify another human...

Had he been wrong about the team having four members?

Or was the last doing a good job of evading him?

Or had just bugged out?

Then a pain akin to a white-hot poker lanced into his stomach.

He looked down in shock, saw the entry wound—even with the thermal imaging goggles on——and immediately his sharply trained body and mind shifted from attack to defence. With the submachine gun in one hand, he clamped the other over the wound. Blood oozed wet and sticky between his fingers.

"Not good," Herron murmured as he took cover behind a tree. "Not good."

He waited a second, then stumbled through the forest, away from the shooter. Within minutes, he was going to be in terrible pain, the adrenaline only able to do so much. A few minutes after that, he'd go into shock. But that was still more time than he'd have if whoever was out there caught up with him or put another bullet in him. He'd fight while he still could.

Pride wouldn't let him stop.

He stumbled and fell to the ground. His mind was fogged with pain and blood loss, but instinct and muscle memory got him back to his feet. He made it a few more yards, had to lean against a tree as he fought off a wave of nausea. He vomited—blood in the fluid—and then caught a flash of colour out of the corner of his eye.

He was a split-second too slow to act.

He screamed in pain as the operative who'd been tracking him jammed the stock of his submachine gun into the bullet wound. It was a perfectly aimed blow and hurt more than the gunshot itself, sending Herron reeling. He stumbled to one knee, unable to catch his breath through the pain.

The operative smashed him in the side of the skull. Herron collapsed.

He was bleeding.

He was in excruciating pain.

He was dying.

Not yet...

He rolled onto his back, tried to aim his submachine gun at the enemy, but his foe was too fast. He kicked out at Herron's hand and dislodged the gun from his weakened grip. It landed in the dirt, and the operative's boot found Herron's mid-section, stomping over and over and over.

Herron screamed in agony and anger, the last outraged exclamation of a life that was almost over. With all the strength he had left, he caught the operative's boot as another kick came in, twisted it. His assailant went down in a heap, his howls loud and lengthy.

With only a second to act, Herron inched closer to the submachine gun. It was a dozen feet away, but in his current state, it may as well have been a dozen miles. Each movement was accompanied by indescribable pain, enough that he might black out at any moment.

But while he was alive, he'd keep fighting.

Eleven feet...

Ten feet...

A breath.

Nine feet...

Eight feet...

He let out a ragged cough, wet and meaty, spat blood on the ground.

Seven feet...

Six feet...

The length of a tall person between him and his target... between him and a chance...

Five feet...

Four feet...

A mighty, urgent scream of determination tore from him.

Three feet...

Two feet...

Almost there.

One foot...

He reached out, clawed at the strap of the weapon, and pulled it closer. Wrapping his hand around its grip, he felt powerful again, like he was the weapon, a blade unsheathed. His life's work was now to kill the enemy operative, even if it meant his own end.

He had a chance. And that's all he had ever needed.

"Ooph."

He grunted as a boot came down on his wrist and pinned the hand and the gun to the ground. The operative stood over him.

"You—"

Pain stole the words from his mouth as the business end of his enemy's submachine gun pressed into his stomach near the bullet wound. A volcano erupted inside his torso, and he clenched his jaw so hard he cracked a tooth.

The operative spoke for the first time. In English. "You interfered in China's business once and got away." He kicked the gun further away from Herron. "Where did he go after Fiji, we wondered. We thought we'd lost you. Lucky for you."

A kick in the stomach.

"But then you interfered again..."

Another kick.

"You critically damaged our smuggling ring and put it out of business. Yet you still weren't happy..."

And another.

"You compromised one of our key people, a woman responsible for putting the Philippine government in our pocket..."

Again.

"You've ruined our influence in Fiji and now the Philippines, but our primary plan remains unaffected."

And again.

"So, instead of gaining influence through control over other governments, we will now shift to gaining influence through control over *you*."

More.

As more blows rained down and the pain overwhelmed him, Herron blacked out. A few times he woke, surprised to be alive, what reserves of brainpower he had left stunned that he could take so much punishment. Stunned, yet firm in the knowledge of one fact.

He would die here.

He coughed. "Kill..."

"We know who you are, Mitch." The operative smiled down at him. "You've drifted through life since you left the United States military. A nuisance, like a fly buzzing here and there..."

"...me."

The operative drove his boot down again, cutting

him off. "But you finally got swatted. And now you're going to face up to your crimes."

Herron's voice was quiet and broken, barely a whisper, as soft as the breeze still blowing through the forest. "Please..."

The operative grinned, a smile of supreme confidence and situational dominance. Herron had worn it himself a hundred times, moments before he snuffed out a foe. Now the shoe was on the other foot.

"Oh no, Mr Herron. If you think you're going to die that easily, you're going to be most disappointed..."

ABOUT THE AUTHOR

Steve P. Vincent is the USA Today Bestselling Author of the Jack Emery and Mitch Herron conspiracy thrillers.

Steve has a degree in political science, a thesis on global terrorism, a decade as a policy advisor and training from the FBI and Australian Army in his conspiracy kit bag.

When he's not writing, Steve enjoys whisky, sports and travel.

You can contact Steve at all the usual places:

stevepvincent.com
steve@stevepvincent.com

ACKNOWLEDGMENTS

Biggest shout out to you — the reader — for your patience. I've seen the emails and the social posts, and I know it took a while.

Boy, a lot happened between the last one and now. My deepest apologies for the delay in getting this story — or any story — to you.

Six months in lockdown because of the coronavirus and a newborn son combined to detonate all my writing schedules.

Back on track now!

Thanks to Gerard and Dave for the beta, Pete for the edits and Stuart for the cover — as always.